Pumpkin Seeds And Other Gifts

Stories from the FEMRITE Regional Writers Residency, 2008

T0316535

Edited by
Helen Moffet
and
Violet Barungi.

FEMRITE PUBLICATIONS LIMITED
KAMPALA

FEMRITE PUBLICATIONS LIMITED
P.O. Box 705, Kampala
Tel: 256-041-543943/0772-743943
Email: info@femriteug.org
www.femriteug.org

ISBN   978-9970-700-22-6

Printed by:

Good News Printing Press Ltd.
Plot 11/13 Nasser Lane Opp. Railways Goodshed
P.O. Box 21228 Kampala, Uganda
Tel: +256 414 344897
E-mail: info@goodnewsprinting.co.ug

Contents

Foreword

In November 2008, by a stroke of the most amazing good fortune, I was invited to facilitate FEMRITE's Regional African Women Writers Residency. In spite of all kinds of apparently insurmountable barriers (such as an expired passport), I somehow made it to Uganda – my first visit to this fascinating and friendly country, where the air smelled of woodsmoke and water.

The residency was magical – no other word for it. The sum of the whole was greater than the parts, as we talked and shared and wrote and were deeply refreshed and inspired. It is not possible to convey the chemistry in the room as we worked together, read each other's writings and supported one another. I have seldom been in a space so gentle, yet so vibrant. It was soul-restoring.

I consider myself deeply honoured to have been entrusted with the task of facilitating a residency with such an astonishingly diverse and talented group of women writers: journalists, teachers, publishers, activists, students, screenwriters, film-makers, academics. There was an excellent mix of youth and maturity, energy and experience, optimism and wisdom. We also received robust and generous support from local academics, religious leaders and even government dignitaries, who visited us, encouraged us, and participated in our readings.

The residency ran like clockwork, thanks to the unfailing efficiency of FEMRITE's staff and members, especially Hilda Twongyeirwe, Lilian Tindyebwa and Brenda Sophie Alal. Our activities and seminars took place in comfort courtesy of the magnificent hospitality of the Kampala International Hotel, with its beautiful views over the inlets and islands of Lake Victoria. I am sure we all gained a few pounds at those delicious buffets featuring local cuisine.

Towards the end of our week together, we read our work to an enthusiastic audience in the lush grounds of Makerere University, a wonderful opportunity to meet other local writers and perform alongside them.

The stories and poems that follow have been selected from those written at the workshop, and we hope you enjoy reading them as much as we enjoyed writing them. Of course, they are only the tip of the iceberg; many of us have found our latent creativity so richly nourished by this residency that we've been writing ever since.

One very strong story written at the residency does not appear here, for technical reasons and reasons of privacy: a brilliant and chilling story of a young girl who tries to lay a charge of rape and is thwarted by the police, by Ethiopian crime journalist, Yemodish Bekele. Yemodish is a very talented writer and I hope to see her story in print one day.

I would like to thank FEMRITE and her sponsors The Commonwealth Foundation and Africalia for affording all of us this blessed opportunity – and blessing it was. But most of all, I am grateful to the amazing women who attended, and who made the residency such a unique success: not just in terms of creative output, but also in activist and inter-regional networking. Each woman who attended represented her country to that country's credit.

So, to my dear sisters – Yemodish Bekele, Mastidia Mbeo, Hilda Twongyeirwe, Lilian Tindyebwa, Brenda Sophie Alal, Kingwa

Kamencu, Olivia Jembere, Colleen Higgs, Yaba Badoe, Betty Mukashema, Winnie Munyarugerero, Constance Obonyo, Philomena Nabweru Rwabukuku, Margaret Ntakalimaze – I thank you for the words you wrote, and the ones you spoke, and for the openness of your minds and hearts.

Helen Moffett, Cape Town 2009

A Girl's Gotta Do What A Girl's Gotta Do

By Kingwa Kamencu

"Mother, you have to take the medicine, whether you like it or not." Njeri spoke in a patronising tone, her voice shrill, as she looked at the old woman lying on the bed. "It's good for you," she added as an afterthought, a plastic smile fixed on her face.

"I'm not sick, for heaven's sake. I merely sprained my ankle, do not got a heart attack!" complained the old lady on the bed, frustration and anger making her strong voice quiver. She was tired of being cosseted and coddled and treated like an invalid.

"Nevertheless, you need the medicine; it will make you rest," her daughter Njeri went on, undeterred by the old lady's outburst. "Drink up, or I'll be forced to resort to extremes," she warned, a malevolent glow coming to her eyes.
"No! I'm not taking any medicine and that's that!" the old lady stubbornly reaffirmed.

Njeri shrugged and rifled unhurriedly through her doctor's bag. She emerged triumphant with an empty syringe and affixed a long evil-looking needle to its end, which she used to draw the medicine from a vial. "You leave me no other choice, Mother," she said, as she plunged the needle into her mother's uncovered left shoulder.

"You miserable child, is this the thanks I get for sending you off to medical school? All that learning so that you can

1

misuse it on your poor old mother! If your father were alive to see this he'd, he'd… he'd…"

At this point, the old lady fell silent, her eyeballs rolled back, her face grew peaceful, and she slumped back on the pillows in a deep slumber, the medicine having taken the desired effect. Njeri smiled coldly as she returned her instruments into the bag, picked it up, and left, not bothering to cover the sleeping form.

When the old lady awoke, it was pitch dark. The luminous hands of the beautiful ornate bedside clock pointed to 3.35 a.m. She remembered the incident with her daughter, and clicked her tongue in disgust at her daughter's cold-heartedness.

That daughter of hers had never been a good sort, what with her cold eyes, hard heart and sharp tongue. She had been the same even in her childhood. She had always refused affection, and as a baby, she would cry when picked up, preferring to be left alone.

"Well, that was through no fault of mine," the old lady muttered to herself.

Her daughter's mistreatment and coldness towards her wasn't the worst of her problems. A diabolical plan had recently been revealed to her, hatched by her own children: her daughter Njeri and two of her three sons. Their father, who had died several years ago, had left a large fortune in her name to distribute among her four children as she saw fit. So far, she had ensured that they had received the best education and basics to get a start in life. The rest of her wealth would be divided at her death through the will she would leave. She now reflected on her children and their present situations.

Her first-born son, Kuria, had opened a bar on the outskirts of Nairobi two years ago. According to her sources, the bar was doing rather badly, as Kuria, a poor manager, failed to keep his records and finances straight. He was apparently in debt, having borrowed money from banks and various friends to provide for his wife and young son. Her second-born son, Kamau, was an enterprising lawyer who never seemed satisfied with the money he earned, even though he had a successful partnership in a law firm. The word "more" was a driving factor in his life.

Njeri, her only daughter, was a practising doctor and though brilliant in mind, she lacked in warmth of heart. She was heartless enough to resort to scheming against her own mother to get her money.

The old lady's thoughts ran to her last-born son, Njenga, and she smiled fondly as she thought of him. He was her favourite of the four, the sunshine after the stormy rain. Njenga was currently studying theology and hoped to become a church minister. He was the only one she deemed completely kind, honest and loving. There was not a bad bone in his entire being; he was the sort that wouldn't hurt a fly.

She pensively replayed the meeting she had had with her lawyer the week before.

"Muthoni, I am sorry to be the one to tell you this, but watch out for your children; the older three especially. They don't have the best of interests regarding your welfare," he had warned her.

Apparently Kuria, Kamau and Njeri had been to see him regarding their father's will. They wanted a share in the family property, which they felt was their due, despite the fact that they were all well over age, working and living independently away from home. Kuria, whose business wasn't doing very well, had

3

seemed to be the head of the gang, as it was he who was most vocal among the three. All three were demanding their share of inheritance out of the property left by their father. The lawyer had tried to explain that their mother, not he, was the one in charge of the family assets, and she could do as she pleased with it. This news had not gone down well, and the three had marched out of his office to deliberate on what to do next.

The following day he had received a phone call from Kuria, who had asked, "And what if the controller of the property is proven to be of unsound mind due to age or other factors, what would happen then?" The lawyer had reflected a second before answering truthfully, "Then other beneficiaries, probably the said person's children, would be named."

Their questions and whole pattern of thinking had unnerved the lawyer, and he had had to summon Muthoni for a meeting to inform her of the sequence of events, and to advise her. She had listened to him solemnly, thanked him, and told him she would have it all under control.

Just as she had been about to put her plan into action, she had gone and sprained her dratted ankle. She had now been bedridden for a week, but fortunately she was improving day by day. She moved her foot and smiled to herself in the pitch darkness. The pain was almost gone. By late morning, she knew she would be hopping around and about, and wouldn't have to be at the mercy of the three ingrates any more. She would be able to carry out her plan before they carried out theirs.

She shuddered at the thought of their evilness. "Do they really plan to prove me mad or of unsound mind just because I'm old?" she wondered out loud. "None among them deserves

4

a penny. They won't get even a single cent from me. I might even leave it all to Njenga, their youngest brother."

The bright noonday sun caressed her slight frame, its warmth spreading into her. She was seated in the back garden, her concentration focused on the gardener hard at work, pruning the leafy hedge. She watched him, all youth and vitality as he concentrated on the task at hand. His muscles rippled and bunched under the white T-shirt he wore – by now reduced to a sweaty dampness. He suddenly noticed her gaze and turned with a friendly wave. "Habari ya mama," he greeted her with a toothy smile before he turned back to his work.

He was a hard worker and had worked for her for two years now. He was honest, respectful, disciplined and loyal. He came from a very humble background, having grown up in the city ghettos and receiving only a scanty education. Currently he seemed happy working for her. Here he received free meals and housing along with decent pay at the end of the month.

Muthoni reviewed her situation. Even though she was still young at heart and in mind, her body was weakening. She had lived her 67 years rather well, though. The problem of her children wanting to take her money without her knowledge could not be solved alone. She watched the gardener still busy with the hedge-clippers, hard at work. "Hmm…" she thought to herself. Cogwheels were moving in her head as a plan formulated.

"Ngugi," she called, beckoning him to approach her. "I'll scratch your back if you'll scratch mine," she was thinking as he took the proffered seat. Muthoni then set out to convince him to be part of her plan.

5

*****

The lawyer was just settling down to his breakfast when his wife came in with the morning newspaper. "Dear, isn't this the old lady you represent, the one you introduced me to the other day in your office?" she asked with a frown, handing him the newspaper and pointing to the large picture filling the front page.

The lawyer took one look at the picture and headline, and guffawed out loud: "BLUSHING BRIDE OF 67 MARRIES 25-YEAR-OLD GARDENER," he read out.

"The old girl sure has outwitted them, hasn't she? She's gotten herself married to that young gardener of hers, forty-two years her junior and all. Well, those wicked children shan't see a penny of the money they were so eager to lay their hands on. I bet she'll change her will and leave it all to the penniless gardener. Just you wait and see."

The lawyer shook his head in fond amusement as he skimmed through the story and admired the picture. It showed old Muthoni and her new husband Ngugi on their wedding day. The bride was a blushing, radiant picture of health and energy, never mind her age.

"Gone out and shocked the whole country, that's for sure. She'll be the talk of the town for weeks."

His wife smiled, indolently nodding in agreement. "True, but you know at the end of it all, a girl's gotta do what a girl's gotta do."

The Secret Cave

By Kingwa Kamencu

Kathure gingerly padded over the stones by the river. She looked behind her, and seeing no one in the vicinity, ducked under the lush green overhanging foliage on the river bank that covered the entrance to their secret cave. She peered through the darkness till her eyes adjusted to the gloom. He hadn't arrived yet; she would have a few minutes to get her jumbled thoughts together. She sat on the cool earth floor and crossed her legs demurely, arranging the shapeless brown calico dress, the usual garb of the village girls, she wore to cover them. She shut her eyes and breathed in the earthy damp smell of the cave, and as she did this, she grew calmer.

A rustling at the entrance jolted her out of her reverie. It was him: tall, handsome Samuel. Her heart pounded faster as he slowly approached her, the burning anger she had felt dissipating. Samuel, her Samuel; everything was perfect about him in her eyes. Everything, apart from the pasty pink colour of his skin, the deep blue of his eyes and the shock of fine blond hair on his head. Samuel was white and she was black. Black and white, white and black: they would never be accepted anywhere. Such liaisons were considered illicit, with couples killed or disinherited: everything discouraged such relationships. Samuel Dobson, son of a Scottish missionary, and Kathure wa Kimathi, daughter of prominent elder Njuri-Ncheke…

7

If anyone found out about them, she would be marked as a sell-out, a traitor, a spy and without much ado, put to death by the fighters in her own village. Treason could not be forgiven. The fighters in the forest, along with most of the village people, despised and distrusted everything about the Whiteman. White skin was an embodiment of evil, death, humiliation, forced backbreaking labour, forced taxation, forced meaningless laws, looting of their land. In short, white skin was the enemy.

Samuel's sturdy boots came to a halt beside her and he crouched low, looking kindly into her face. He gathered her work-hardened dark brown hands into his own pale soft ones. "I'm sorry. I'm very sorry. I heard about what happened to Mugambi. I wish I could have done something, anything, but I couldn't."

Tears sprang to her eyes. Why was he being kind? She had planned to lash out at him. He and his kind had captured her brother Mugambi on the charge of being a Mau Mau. They had hanged him the previous day on the 'Mau Mau tree' to serve as a warning to others. Kathure could still see Mugambi's lifeless body swinging forlorn and stiff in the cold wind. She hadn't cried yesterday, but now she couldn't hold back the tears.

"Why Mugambi, why him?" she sobbed against Samuel.

She cried for Mugambi, and for the insanity of what was happening all around them; she cried for the other friends she had lost in the forest; her captured relatives, some dead and others languishing in pain, at the area D.O, enduring constant torture of the whereabouts of others in the forest. Kathure cried also for a love that would never blossom, never be lived out: the futility of her and Samuel.

8

Samuel gathered her to himself, stroking her plaited hair as her slight frame shook in anguish.

Why Mugambi? Why Mugambi of the ever-cheerful smile, of the kind word for everyone, and the gentlest of hearts? He was his mother's favourite, his sister's loyal ally and his father's pride. At 24, he was in his prime. Not particularly eager to join the fighting, but it would have been shameful for his family if he had stayed behind when all his age-mates had gone to the forest to fight. Now he was gone, forever. He'd never tease Kathure mercilessly about her beaus, protect her from their mother's acidic tongue, or bring her little treats from the market. No more Mugambi.

"Why didn't you do something to help him?" she cried at Samuel, knowing the answer even before he spoke it.
"You know I couldn't. Questions would be asked. Your people would kill both of us if they ever found out about us."

"This is senseless. Why does it have to be this way? Why all this fighting and killing? Why can't we love one another in the open?"

He shook his head. "I don't have the answers either; I guess that's just how things are. But they won't always be so."
She drew in a ragged breath and extricated herself from his embrace. "We can't see each other again. We have to end this, it's useless, it has no future. We shouldn't have begun it in the first place." He nodded silently, his heart heavy at the finality of her tone.

She darted towards the cave's exit, turning back to take one last look at him. "Thank you, Samuel, for everything" were her last words as she disappeared.
He flopped down, leaning against the cave wall. She was gone.

He would be going too, back to Scotland to finish his education. There was no point in staying around. His father wanted him to become a missionary like himself, but he knew he wouldn't. He wanted to leave the lush Nyambene hills, with their secret caves and memories of a beautiful Meru girl far, far away. No more dreamy secret caves, no more stolen hours and illegal trysts for him. He was going back to reality. He had no other option.

The Cradle

By Kingwa Kamencu

I know the story of how
She had once been
The cradle of all humankind,
The genesis of all living and breathing,
The birth-ground of all empire.
But then in time,
Things had fallen apart.

But I've been watching and waiting
And reading the signs
And they all tell me
That the cradle is once again pregnant
Heavy,
Ready to deliver
Any time soon.

I see it in the way
Those children inside her stir,
Move, foment, seethe,
With the pain of being inside
In that watery dark for far too long.
A watery dark they have been stuck into,
Pegged in, enclosed around, hemmed into,
Trapped down in, shoved upon, condemned to,
Misled, misinformed, and

Hoodwinked for far too long.
They know they must get out now,
Get away from the suffocation and bleakness inside.
These days, you see,
They have their learning; they have seen other worlds
Sniffed the tangy possibility of new vistas
They know who they are
What they want
And they will take no less.

I see it in the way
Those children kick,
Jerk about, lash out, thrash against,
Refuse, demur, dissent,
Hit against the inner enemies as well,
Refuse to be stifled,
After all these years.
After numerous struggles
From the war trenches to the academies,
To the literary battle fronts,
They have never given up.

She's been pregnant a long time now
Fifty years and counting
It's crossing to the abnormal, the surreal,
The absurd
Her belly is bulging, distended, grotesque.
All she does now is sit in her corner
Of the world's lounge
Legs propped up on a white coffee table

Rendered still, immobile
As she watches her six other sisters
Dance, sashay and flourish,
Run from one corner to another
Tut-tut at her, stuff her sick with solutions for her condition,
As they rule
The world.

Her legs are swollen,
Her blood pressure's high,
Oedema, they say it is.
She is besieged by fainting spells.
She's been haemorrhaging from inside,
So much blood has flowed out
From between her heavy thighs,
Her body has been one big war zone.

I closed my eyes,
Unable to understand how a being could bear
Such a torturous existence.
But when I opened them again,
She had delivered!

And out of her watery dark womb,
What a sight to behold:
Fat, gurgling, cherub-cheeked babies,
Round and luscious, black skins gleaming.
Gone were the pathetic skin-and-bone tots
Staring out of wide vacant eyes, flies nibbling at their corners,
BBC, CNN, long packed up and trotted off to the great wildebeest

migration
In search of the new exotic
Real African picture.

Abundantly stocked hospitals,
Professional world-class doctors,
Nobel Prize-winning scientists, economists, artists,
All home-grown and home-retained
All out of the fruit of her womb!

Green lush farms thriving, maize, wheat, banana, tea, coffee
Bursting at their seams,
Excesses generating energy,
All self-sufficient and dignified,
Well-fed, sated.
Picturesque little cozy houses set amidst the luscious green,
Enough for everyone's need,
Having done away with greed.
No more polythene-paper houses, tin-shack slums, tented IDP
camps,
Matchbox dwellings, flying toilets,
No more victims to the elements.
The disease, poverty, ignorance triad sorted.

I cried out in surprise,
Wonder and delight at this.
Was this possible, could it actually be?

But I blinked.
And when I opened my eyes,

She was still pregnant
Flailing her arms and legs,
Rolling her neck from side to side,
Moaning in pain and anguish
Like before.

And it made me sit and wonder,
What will it take
For this glorious, blessed cradle
To give birth once again?

The Pumpkin Seed

By Hilda Twongyeirwe Rutagonya

There is a faint knock somewhere. Kokokoko... kokokoko... I wonder whether it is my mind pounding from last night's noise. I close my eyes tight and try to shut it out, but it is persistent. Kokokoko... kokokoko... It sounds close. Kokokoko... kokokoko... kokokoko... It gets loud. Kokokoko... kokokoko! It is like the woodpecker deep in a dark and hushed forest. Kokokoko... kokokoko! I wonder what time of the night it is. Or is it morning already?

Disturbed out of my slumber, I stretch but my arms hit something next to the bed. It is a chair. I am in a strange room. Then I remember it is my new home. It is my husband's house. I stretch out to wake him but my arm rests on cold bed sheets. Streaks of dim light steal into the room through the window across the room. The knocking halts. I breathe with relief and turn and face the wall. I want to sleep some more. Then it starts again. Kokokoko... it is louder... kokokoko...closer... kokokoko!

Slowly, I raise my head and listen more attentively, but my eyes remain shut. Kokokoko! Kokokoko! I open my eyes and I realise that the knocking is at my husband's house, on our door. I wonder who is knocking and why. It is only one day after my wedding and I desperately need to sleep a little bit longer. Kokokoko. I decide I will not move an inch until whoever is knocking gets tired and leaves.

My wedding had been such a tiring affair that I would

17

really appreciate being left alone to rest. If my husband did not feel as tired, that is okay. After all, I did most of the preparations. I could have left him to take on the bulk of it, but most of what he did turned out to be disastrous. George can make your nose twitch sometimes! Like our wedding cards. Cheap, colourless, tiny! To him, the card was the most insignificant part of the wedding. Something that people wouldn't even look at a second time. A paper that would just litter the wedding reception venue the following day! To me, the wedding invitation card was our wedding souvenir.

My wedding gown was another issue. "I think you are just fussing, Lyn. Who cares about the wedding gown? You are so beautiful and people will be looking at you and not the gown," he had said. I had worked so hard, dieting and exercising in order to come up with a wedding-size figure that would look stunning in a gown. And so there was no room for negotiation over the gown. I did not even take a second look at it, the evening he trudged home with it, for me to try on. He tried to explain that it was a wedding contribution from his cousin: "Look! She charged us only fifty per cent of what she charges others. And my cousin looked really good in this gown. Just try it on. Try it on."

I would not listen. Honestly, he should have known that fashions change! His cousin had wedded over ten years before! And really, people have different tastes. I was not about to wear that huge and shapeless gown. I just stood my ground, and we had to book another gown to my taste. In the process we lost the fifty per cent amount George had already paid. The receipt from his cousin was clear: Money once paid is not refundable. And what a tight budget we had! The cousin claimed we had made her miss a customer, one who had wanted the dress for that very weekend. "For that matter, I am sorry but I cannot make any refunds." the cousin insisted. "This of course does not mean that I do not feel for my cousin. I know he is doing his best to organise this wedding. And that is why I had offered my gown. But it is understandable that Lyn does not find it suitable. No ill feelings of course." No ill feelings indeed but I would have agreed with her better if she had accompanied her words with actions as Jesus would say – faith without actions...

Kokokoko... the knocker is not moving away. And where is my husband? He must have left the bed so carefully as not to wake me up. But he should have left the door open. I smile to myself, remembering some of Jeffrey Archer's and Sydney Sheldon's novels of romance that I had combed while in high school and even at University. It dawns on me that my husband had left the bed on the first day of our marriage without kissing me good morning. He had left without reminding me that our hearts belonged together.

I had looked forward to many first things of marriage. The first morning was one of them. I had mused about what we would say to each other after waking up, about who would wake up first in our matrimonial bed and what we would do at waking up.

As I turn and roll on cold bed-sheets, I wonder whether it would have been the same if we had spent the night in a hotel room in the city. I wonder what it would have been if we had flown to another country on honey moon. I want to pull my notebook and make note of my first morning as Mrs .... I then remember that I have neither a pen nor a notebook.

We had travelled all the way from the city to have

our wedding in his home town. He had insisted on it, and I had relented. "We have such a big family. Please give me the opportunity to honour them with a wedding."

Indeed so many people had turned up for the wedding; so many to greet and smile at... so many to talk to and listen to. "This is your sister-in-law. Her grandmother is married to the grandfather of my sister-in-law. This is your son. His great-grandfather was a blood-brother to my great-grandfather. This is your mother-in-law too. Her mother is a sister to my uncle's wife." So many faces popping up left, right and centre to welcome the bride. And so many nitty-gritty items to see to, despite the fact that I was a bride and in a new environment. By the time my husband and I went to bed, we were too exhausted to remember that it was our wedding night. I did not even remember to recite him the poem I had written as my wedding gift to him.

I had had the poem framed, wrapped and hidden from him, to be unwrapped on our wedding night! I feel a bit embarrassed to think that I never remembered it at all. As a consolation I recite it to myself:

We

I
And
You.

I sat on a stone
You sat on a stump
Valleys and hills between
Our hearts leapt.

They leapt high and higher
Shooting through the moon
And there
Behind there
They got intertwined.

Pulling out of either
Instead getting tighter
They burst into either
But forming neither

Flying back in awe
Floating lower and lower
One heart returned

Mine did not
Nor did yours
But ours did.

I ceased to be
You ceased to be
We became

We.

The incessant knocker is not about to give up. Kokokoko...
kokokoko! I am wide awake now. I jump out of bed and head
towards the wall to switch on the light, but then I remember
there is no electricity. The trees and banana plantation around
the home keep the house dark. Kokokoko... kokokoko! My
head is still buzzing with the pampala... pampala... pampala
of the after-party disco. Using a torch, I locate the green and
yellow kitenge Aunt J had given me as a wedding present. It

is warm and soft. Aunt J is my favourite aunt. A passionate seventy-year-old woman who sounds and looks every inch in her mid-forties!

I wrap myself in the six-yard kitenge and head for the door. Outside the door stands my mother-in-law. One hand is on her hip, while the other is bearing a calabash shoulder-high. I wonder what she is carrying, and suspect it might be millet porridge for me. I want to joke and tell her that I do not drink cold things early in the morning, but I notice that just like me, she does not seem to be in the mood to talk.

Before I speak, my sister-in-law approaches us. She is balancing a hoe on her shoulder. I am not sure what this is all about. Further away, in one corner of the compound, my husband is standing with his father. I don't quite make out what they are talking about, but they are looking at us.

"Good morning," I greet the women, kind of grudgingly.

"Good morning, Mugole," my sister-in-law responds. I had already been told that people would call me bride even for years after my wedding. Mugole means bride and it is a respectful way of referring to new wives. I don't think my mother-in-law responds. I do not hear her. So I greet her again. She mumbles and I feel queer. I want to go back into the house and brush my teeth. But I remain standing. I feel captive.

"You look sleepy," my sister-in-law says.

"Yes," I respond.

"We are sorry we woke you up. But it's not very early, is it? People are already up and down. Women are already up the hills, sowing millet," she continues. I want to ask her why she herself is not up some hill doing the same. My adrenaline is rising. I want to ask her whether she does not eat millet. But I shut up. I am a bride. I am her brother's bride. I wonder why my husband is not with me. Whether he is an accomplice to whatever is going on.

My mother-in-law calls a little girl in the compound. Shanita comes running. She asks her to bring some water. Shanita sprints to the mud-and-wattle kitchen and returns with a small jerrycan.

"Here is the water, Kaka. I have brought it. I fetched it from the well yesterday evening."
"Shanita has a good hand. When she touches things, they respond well."

"Even when I plait my friend's hair it grows faster," Shanita bats in and smiles again.

"We have not asked you about hair," her grandmother interrupts her. Shanita smiles, unconcerned about her grandmother's remarks. She is excited. Whatever we are about to do must be tickling her. She sounds mature for her age. She is of slight build, wears an oversized sweater with sleeves that stretch over her hands. She looks at me and smiles, her eyes dancing between me and the small jerrycan in her hands. I think she is a warm girl.

"Come with us," my mother-in-law finally addresses me. I want to ask where we are going, but I don't. I am a bride. I keep quiet. She is my mother-in-law. So I turn and follow. I pray that my kitenge holds firm because I am not quite properly dressed. I did not know we were moving away from the house, so I did not put on any undergarments.

I hope these people are not taking me to dig. It's only a day after my wedding. I am not supposed to go to the garden until my parents have performed the out-of-door ritual where they invite relatives and ask me to dance with my husband in front of everybody. They would then perform a mock ceremony, removing a headscarf from my head as an indication that I was now uncovered to go and carry out any duties required of a wife outside the house. They would also give me gifts, including a hoe as a symbol for all other farm and home implements implying that I was now released to go and work.

From the home we walk in a line. We are silent. My mother-in-law leads the way. She is still balancing the calabash on her left palm. I am curious about the contents of the calabash. But whatever it is, it does not look heavy. My sister-in-law follows. The hoe hangs precariously on her right shoulder. A cheeky thought steals into my mind. I wish the hoe would tilt over and cut into her small heels. That would be a perfect excuse to put an end to the morning pilgrimage. But she walks on, stepping very lightly as if she is weightless. Shanita follows, swinging the jerrycan of water from one hand to the other. She is giggling and making indecipherable signs to several other children that now litter the compound behind us. The wedding excitement seems to have rubbed off on everybody, making them wake up early.

We snake through the banana plantation, past avocado and mango trees, and past lush pumpkin gardens and coffee trees heaving heavily with green-purple coffee beans. Briefly I breathe in the refreshing sight and walk on. A cold wind blows on my ears and my nose twitches. My blood is boiling higher with each step! I stretch my neck to look into the calabash, but my mother-in-law is a giant. All I see is the soft brown hue of the back of the calabash.

I wonder why I am trudging on, deeper into the shamba. I feel like an idiot. My mind dashes back to my bridal shower. No one had warned me about this. Aunt J had told me many things I could expect from my in-laws, like my sister-in-law borrowing my best outfit when we both have a party to attend. Many things my husband expected from me, like letting him believe he is right when both of us know he is wrong. Many things to do, like capturing my husband's heart by attending to his stomach, and many things not to do, such as facing the wall when we are in bed together. Aunt J had told me many dos and don'ts of marriage, but she had not mentioned the morning walk.

Suddenly, the leader of the group stops in her tracks and we all stop, almost bumping into each other. She turns off the footpath into the weeds and shrubs on our left. We follow. The brown and green gomesi she is wearing sways in the morning breeze and mingles with the blown earth and the weeds. She becomes one with them.

"Here," she says, interrupting my thoughts. "This is a fertile area and we welcome you to this family." She smiles, but just as my face is beginning to warm up to her smile, her lips return to form a small oval shape. I want to say that the welcome should not be in the bush, but instead other words form.

"Thank you for welcoming me so warmly," I respond as I hug the kitenge round my wedding-size body to keep away the cold.

"You now belong to our family," she continues. "From now on you will be called Bahirwa, because you are a very blessed woman to have attracted the attention of the Basingo clan. Bahirwa is your pet name and that is how you will be called by members of the family."

25

I want to hug her in sisterhood and tell her that she and I are not Basingo. Instead, I hug my kitenge closer.

Shanita smiles. She tilts her head shyly and cups her mouth in her small hands to hide the smile.

"You will like this family," my mother-in-law continues.

"If you choose to," my sister-in-law adds with a smile.

I am now very curious about the contents of the calabash. As if to answer my thoughts, my mother-in-law lowers the calabash and steps closer to me. "These are pumpkin seeds. Please pick one and plant it. Pick any that pleases your eyes," she says as she lowers the calabash further.

Surprised, I pick one seed. It is light. It is insignificant. It is a pumpkin seed.

"This is the beginning of your journey in this home, in this clan. Now plant it here," she says, indicating a place near my feet.

My sister-in-law, who had up to now held the hoe tightly on her shoulder, casts it in my direction.

The girl in my marrow wants to get hold of the hoe and chuck it into the nearest bush. The bride in me wants to put the seed back in the calabash and smile to the cameras. I am still celebrating my wedding.

"Shall we?" my mother-in-law asks, interrupting my thoughts. I hold the hoe firmly to steady my shaking spirit and I dig a hole in the ground. I throw the seed in the hole and stretch my hand towards the calabash for another seed. My mother-in-law moves the calabash away and shakes her head.

"You have finished your task, my daughter. You plant only one seed."

Shanita steps forward and waters the seed. She pours so much water that it forms a small river that flows towards my feet. I do not move. My feet block the water instead and it forms a small puddle below me. A lake forms in my mind. I want to pull everybody so we can all a have a swim. The puddle slowly seeps into the soil and my lake evaporates.

"But suppose the one seed dries up or fails to germinate?" I finally find my tongue.

"That's the point, my daughter. The pumpkin seed is like a woman. It is either productive or worthless," she says and smiles. This time the smile lingers on a little longer until I look away. A lump stands stiff in my throat. I want to put my hand and remove the lump. I want to scatter the ground and expose the seed to birds. I want to tell my new family that I need no pumpkin seed to prove the woman in me. But would anyone care to listen?

Three days later I retrace my steps to water my seed. Shanita jumps to accompany me, but I shoo her off. I need to be alone.

At the site, I squat carefully and open the ground. My forehead wets with perspiration. The seed smiles invitingly. I smile back. Reluctantly I reach for her and crush her into pieces. Each piece purges a piece of my soul.

I float back home like a dove from Noah's errand.
Several days pass by and we wait; they, impatiently for the woman I will be; I, patiently for the woman I am.

By The Nile

By Hilda Twongyeirwe Rutagonya

The sun shines softly, warming my forehead
A calm breeze blows past, into lush maize fields across
Serene Nile waters gently descend the slope
Mischievously diving into hide-and-seek to trace their past
Quickly, they all race the steep rocks of Bujagali
Here ... sucking in a yellow jerrycanned melancholic local boy
There ... wrestling a rafted anxious tourist

The waters rejoin and rise in jubilation
Waves clap hands and jump in wild excitement
Shiny bubbles mix and burst into smiling divers
I reach for my Nile bottle and share the spirit of Africa.

22 November 2008

You Are One

By Hilda Twongyeirwe Rutagonya

It is the Lawyer's turn to speak
He is asking me
        "Describe the encounter"
The Magistrate is reading my lips
I wait for him to protest
To overrule the demented Lawyer
Then he speaks
        "Answer the question put to you, will you!"
A chill snakes my spine
        "Liar!"
My strength tumbles
My pride crushes and piles on my feet
My eyes close
I watch them all from behind my pupils
Their irate knees pin me to the ground
Repugnant mouths close in on mine
Dirty hands urgently desecrate my crumbling body
They are tearing into me
A thousand pieces of pain set me on fire
I scream
My voice is stuck in my throat
I am alone
The cold floor beneath is indifferent.

Nov 2008: Inspired by Yemodish's story

For You Mama

By Hilda Twongyeirwe Rutagonya

No brother! Let me – oh!
Let my tears freely flow
For inhibitions stifle my weak body
And the suppressed tears
They flow back to the heart
Making it terribly hurt
No brother, let me, oh!
Let my tears freely flow.

Brother, don't confuse me about reality
When nothing is no longer real
When my clear sight sees but only gray
When my hands clasp but only shells
No brother, let me, oh
Let my tears freely flow.

Brother, don't mystify life
Life is just life - simple
Life is not lifelessness
Life walks
It does not lie in a box
A dark sealed box!
Life breathes
It is not stuffed with cotton wool and all
Oh don't you know what life is?

Brother
Life is Mama and I fight and hug
It is you and I quarrel and dance
Life shouts, screams and runs
Life smiles, giggles and laughs
Life winks, winces and jumps
Life is so full of life! Brother!
Or don't you know life?

Brother,
Let my tears freely flow
For this life that has lost life
This life that lies lifeless.

Ancestors

By Yaba Badoe

Sheba Patterson was what is usually regarded as a 'roots' sister; she was head over heels in love with Africa. Even though her fascination with woven textiles and abstract face masks encouraged her, at times, to view the continent as the most glorious shopping destination in the world, she was right in believing that she was happiest in the birthplace of her ancestors.

A fleeting glance in her direction confirmed Sheba's cultural orientation: nappy hair twirled in chunky twists; a smudge of Egyptian kohl around dark, seductive eyes, and flowing from an ample frame; voluminous, sensual fabrics that flattered her curves – so that when she strolled through campus, she seemed to sashay, sucking in the air around her. Not that she intended to draw attention to herself. She just couldn't help it. She moved in such a way that the easy roll of her hips heralded her namesake: Sheba, lover of Solomon, a king wise enough to succumb to the charms of an extraordinarily intelligent woman.

So, when Ms Patterson came across an invitation a sabbatical in a place of higher learning in West Africa. She thought about it carefully. She weighed the pros and cons of uprooting herself from her home for a year abroad: a year in a country she visited regularly in her dreams. Sheba thought long and hard, and eventually, yielding to a profound desire for prolonged immersion in a place she pined for, she made the necessary arrangements; and within six months, was teaching a course in African-American women writers at the University of Ghana, Legon.

Sheba had never been happier than during those first weeks. The tree-lined campus with its white, red-roofed buildings appeared attractive. The heat, though occasionally oppressive, brought out the copper highlights in her bronze skin. She glowed with good health and contentment, and when she caught her reflection smiling back at her in the mirror, she was in awe that an inner alignment she sensed, but was unable to articulate coherently, having burnished her image, made her eyes brim with deep pools of love.

Convinced she had made the right decision, Sheba uprooted herself once again. She moved from the university campus to a two-bedroomed apartment off East Cantonments Road, popularly known as Oxford Street – the most exhilarating venue in the centre of Accra – and used her hard-earned savings to settle in.

She fashioned curtains from dramatic Woodin prints; she ordered a set of cane furniture from a roadside vendor; then, after decorating her new abode with mirrors and tasteful, colourful artefacts purchased through Aid to Artisans, Sheba acquired a car and finally felt complete.

She had never been better, more ebullient, or at ease; yet behind the bright smiles that she sprinkled like stardust on her colleagues, a vague problem niggled. Sheba had not been paid. The necessary letter had been written to the Registrar through the Head of Department, the requisite copy had been sent to the Head of Salaries, but first one month, then a second ended without a slip in her pigeonhole to assure her that she had been reimbursed for her services.

To begin with, Sheba dismissed the delay as the result of the usual teething problems inherent in a vast, unwieldy bureaucracy. After all, her name had just been placed on the university payroll. It seemed like only yesterday that she'd jumped the hurdles put in her way to open an account at the Osu branch of Barclays Bank. The same thing could have happened back home – that long, agonising wait for remuneration. This was what she told herself. But when the second month merged into a third, and Christmas, with its endless enticements of gifts and consumption loomed ahead, Sheba began to wonder if what she had shrugged off as a mild dose of inefficiency wasn't, in fact, a major case of gross ineptitude.

Direct and open at all times, she expressed her grievance to friends and colleagues alike. Calls were made, another letter was written to Salaries, and to extract what was due to her from the arcane machinery of the nation's premier university, Sheba became a regular visitor to the department. She walked down corridors without end; she knocked on gnarled wooden doors, and spoke to wizened, old men behind desks stacked high with folders and files. Sheba wanted her money, and she was going to get it: even if it meant orchestrating a one-woman sit-in in the office of the person responsible for the delay.

She acted in good faith, unaware of the labyrinthine nature of the flow of cash within a gigantic institution: the dams and eddies, the many streams and tributaries, which, akin to the never-ending Tano river, wind from the Brong Ahafo heartland to the magical Nzema coast, where oil-slicks appear one day, only to disappear the next. Sheba knew none of this. What she did know was that without a regular salary to augment her savings, she was living well beyond her means.

35

Christmas came in its festive glory and hanging on its fairy lights, Jarred Greenshield arrived for the New Year. Jarred, Sheba's long-term boyfriend, gave the impression of being delectably handsome, thanks to the elegant accoutrements with which he adorned himself. His wide, sensual mouth was lined with signs of laughter, as were his eyes; and his short greying hair, shaved close to his head, marked him out as a member of the executive class. He was, in fact, the marketing manager of an advertising company.

He complimented Sheba's profound attachment to the land of her ancestors by being mildly sceptical of her explorations. While she was passionate, he was wryly detached. Indeed, he laughed out loud when she mentioned the aggravation she'd endured because of her unpaid salary.

"Welcome to the Third World," he chortled. The couple were lying naked in bed at Elmina Beach Hotel, having reacquainted themselves with the elusive nooks and crannies of their bodies.

"This ain't no laughing matter, Jarred. I want my money."

"You and me both, honey. Ever thought to consider, they may be taking you for a ride?"

"They wouldn't do that!"

"This is the world, Sheba – the real world."

"You just said it was the Third World!"

"Whichever world we're in, you can't live without money."

Sheba sighed as her fingers trailed down a vein that ran down Jarred's long shapely arm.

"If I were you," he chuckled, "I'd give them something,

36

a little incentive to make them smile. Believe you me, within an hour you'll have all the money that's owed you, and then some."

"You crazy or something? That's bribery, Jarred. And it's my money, after all. I ain't going to give no backhander to get what's rightfully mine!"

"Well, it's your call, Sheba. I guess you'll do what you got to do."

Whether it was Jarred's brief visit that emboldened her, or their visit to Elmina Castle later that morning, Sheba would never know. She had visited Goree Island on one of her trips to Senegal, so she appreciated what was in store for her. However, a chill entered her bones the moment she stepped in the castle's glistening white forecourt. And as she meandered through the dungeons, she felt the weight of her ancestry interrupt the flow of blood in her veins. Red corpuscles buckled, forming the shape of a tearful sickle moon on a cold night. It blocked capillaries and drained lubrication from her bones, so that when she reached the final holding-place of her ancestors and stared through the Door of No Return to the sea beyond, Sheba knew. She understood where she was coming from and where she was heading.

To say that Sheba was thrilled with delight when, on her return to the university, she saw a pay-slip lying in her pigeonhole, is not an overstatement. She danced in jubilation and sang with joy. Then she called Barclays Bank to make sure that the rightful amount had arrived in her account.

"These things take time," the manager warned her. She should give it a day or so. But the following week, when Sheba called again, the money had still not arrived.

What would Zora and Maya and Toni do? Sheba wondered, conjuring up the spirits of her favourite writers – the authors she revered and taught in her classes. What would they do to get what was owed them? After all, she wasn't running a charity. Even Peace Corps volunteers were paid for services rendered.

Sheba ventured, once again, to the office she had visited so often. This was her ninth visit. She walked down the corridor, and after knocking on the second door on the right, walked in without waiting for a response. Mr Algernon Albert Addo (better known as 'Triple A' to his friends) was sitting at his desk, his red-rimmed eyes magnified by an ancient pair of large blue spectacles. He grinned knowingly at the woman before him.

"Ms Patterson," he moaned. "And to what do I owe the pleasure of your company today?"

"Mr Addo," Sheba began, waving her pay-slip in the air.

"I've been paid. I thank you for everything you've done to make that possible. However, the money owed me by the university hasn't reached my account. Where is it?" Sheba snarled.

"How possible?" Mr Addo opened a thick fat ledger that held the intricate details and secrets of his hidden world. He thumbed through it, flipping over pages, and then ran a knotted finger down a list of names, until he found what he was looking for.

"You bank at Osu, don't you, young lady?"
Sheba rarely tolerated being referred to as a "young lady" at the best of times. Today, she bit her tongue.

"Yes," she answered tersely.
"At the Ghana Commercial Bank, Osu?"

"I told you three months ago, Mr Addo, my account is at Barclays."

"Well, that explains it," the man replied, a self-satisfied smile playing on his lips. "We've made a dreadful mistake. I humbly apologise to you for any inconvenience we have caused."

If humility had had anything to do with it, Sheba might not have found it so difficult to accept the apology of a haggard middle-aged man approaching retirement. If Mr Addo had tried to appear sincere, she might have taken Jarred's advice and discreetly offered him an "incentive". But far from looking apologetic, the hardened bureaucrat seemed to be gloating at the myriad impediments in Sheba's path, clearly relishing his power, revelling in it like a bird sipping from a precious pool of rainwater. He smirked while Sheba spluttered, convinced she had given the correct name and address of her bank. Indeed, she knew that she had watched the man write it down in his ledger.

The more he grinned, contradicting her words, the more determined Sheba became not to give in to him. Jarred's advice be damned! She was her own woman and despite every obstacle placed in her way, she would eventually get her money.

That very day, she travelled to the Commercial Bank at Osu, with a letter from the university. The bank was to return the money paid into a fictitious account in her name to the university forthwith. The day after the cheque had been delivered by courier, Sheba was instructed to go back to Mr Addo's office at two o' clock on Friday afternoon, to pick up her salary.

Everything went according to plan. Thursday arrived and Sheba spoke to Mr Addo, who assured her that he would be waiting for her. If by chance he wasn't around, his superior, Mr Abbam, would hold on to the cheque and make sure that she got it.

At two o' clock on Friday, Sheba knocked on Mr Addo's door one last time. He was nowhere to be seen.

"Ah, it's Friday," a secretary in a yellow dress shrugged. She looked tired, harassed, determined to finish a pile of typing on her desk. Nevertheless, sensing Sheba's dismay, she heaved herself up from the desk, revealing that she was in a late stage of pregnancy, and led Sheba down a corridor to Mr Abam's office.

Two men were sitting in the waiting room, browsing through The Daily Graphic and The Times newspapers. They shook their heads when asked if Mr Abam was in. "He's travelled to a funeral. It's Friday," the taller of the two replied. Close to tears, Sheba took a deep breath. Then, summoning up the spirits she loved, begging them to bear witness to her predicament, she called them one after the other: those that had stayed behind and those that had been sent away. She needed their presence to make her last stand.

"I want my money," Sheba cried. "I haven't been paid for over three months, yet I come to work every single day. God knows how I survived Christmas and the New Year without a pay-cheque. Is it fair?" she demanded. "Would you put up with it? How in kingdom come am I supposed to pay my rent, feed myself, put petrol in my car? Tell me, how am I supposed to live without money?"

The two men and the secretary in front of them shook their heads, murmuring a series of sympathetic "Aaahs". "Oh, mobo!" they added, their lips pursed in indignant ovals of astonishment. "You see? Frustration!"

The taller man clapped his hands together. "Look at this poor woman," he tut-tutted. "Righteous anger! Woman work hard, yet they pay her no money? This place no good, no fair. Always, big frustration!"

They chipped in, a conciliatory Greek chorus, affirming Sheba's tirade with gentle pouts of commiseration, little nods of agreement, so that somehow, the stranger in their midst didn't cross the line between anger and fury. She didn't say, "You people have a mountain to climb before you get anywhere." She didn't squeeze her lips and turn her back on them, asserting that they were hurtling recklessly down a path to nowhere. Their eyes held Sheba while their sympathy flowed through her, allowing her to give vent to a seething mass of exasperation.

So when her tirade finally came to an end and the pregnant woman stepped forward with the words, "Madam, we are very sorry. Please forgive us because we love you," Sheba remembered what she already knew. She was where she wanted to be for a reason. She would collect her money on Monday.

Devils On Horseback

By Yaba Badoe

"I remember so many things," the woman whispered.

She was being interviewed by a researcher from Amnesty International. The woman was young, no older than thirty at the most. She was from Eastern Chad, close to the border with Sudan.

The researcher's tape-recorder was running. The woman paused, then continued talking - at first hesitantly, then quickly - releasing her words as though if she dared pause to think, they would escape her.

"I don't want to remember," she went on, "but I can't help myself. You see, when it started, we all seemed to get on well. But then horsemen came from a neighbouring village. They came to the market, upset the stalls and called us Kaffirs. They harassed and frightened us.

"This went on for a year. Then thirty or forty of them came at the same time: devils on horseback with guns. They burnt our houses and stole our cattle. They killed seven of our men. They took all my husband's livestock and we ran away. But my husband went looking for his herd. He promised to meet me at the next village. I waited with our daughter for one day, two days. He didn't return, so I brought my daughter here.

"But the things I have seen, my sister! Those men on horseback, those devils who turned our village into a river of blood; the things I have seen, that I don't want to remember..."

As the woman spoke, her womenfolk surrounded her in a

protective shield of shared emotion. Her words brought tears to their eyes, and when she started weeping, they wept with her for all they had lost: for all they would never forget.

Death In Kismayo

By Yaba Badoe

In memory of Aisha Ibrahim Dhuhulow, who was stoned to
death in Kismayo on 27 October 2008

To begin with, they claimed you were twenty-three.
Then your father explained that you were big for your age.
You were slow, big-boned with the breasts of a woman,
But you were still a child.
Only thirteen.

You lived with your aunt, your father told us on the radio.
Then she described, how, the day before it happened,
You had been raped.
You pointed them out.
Three men.
So she took you to the police station.
But to her surprise the police put you in jail instead.
In Kismayo.
The next day, they accused you of adultery,
and sentenced you to death.
They carried you, screaming and kicking, to a hole
they had dug for you;
"What do you want from me?" you cried.
"What do you want?"
As they buried you up to your neck
people surged forward,

"This isn't justice," someone shrieked. "She is but a child."
But the militants fired in the crowd,
and yet another child died, before,
in front of a thousand witnesses
they stoned you to death in Kismayo.

"What do you want from me?"
I heard your cry in Ghana, Aisha.
We heard you all around our continent,
in every corner of the world we hear you.
And in reply we ask: "What do they want from us?"
That we should cover ourselves to hide their shame?
That we should bow down to embrace their sin,
their filthy secrets of defilement?
And in case we point accusing fingers at those three men
and others like them,
we should let them murder us?

Then let them come for each and every one of us!
Mothers and wives, sisters, daughters, lovers and friends.
But not you, Aisha, not you.
You were just a child
in Kismayo.

Missing Horses

By Colleen Higgs

My father's hands were big and tanned
the backs covered in dark hair
he was a sportsman
good at polo, golf, squash, darts, tennis
a man with exceptional eye-hand co-ordination
and he could draw horses
from memory

in the second half of his life
he missed horses, every day,
horses were his inner life
he yearned for horses, to be among them
to ride them
to smell the hot sweat of horse after a polo match
to hold soft leather reins in his hands again

my father only once ever laid a hand on me
he wasn't given to hidings
he wasn't an affectionate man either, not to me
I loved him because I knew
how sad he was about the horses –
my mother made him choose
it's either me or the horses, she said

Blaming Lulu

By Colleen Higgs

Kate loves to draw. "I'm a drawer. You're a writer," she says. She draws pictures of herself and of me and her father and the dog and her friends. When she shows me the pictures, I wait for her to tell me what she has drawn. I rely on her to interpret for me, to translate. "This is a plate of cupcakes. Here's a shark and a monster. This is Barbie." She loves Barbie best – a golden-haired goddess, princess, fairy godmother, close friend, alter ego.

And then there's Lulu, her 45-year-old inherited doll. Lulu is always the one to blame. She drops and spills and breaks things, she is badly behaved and angry and has mumps and no friends, and is left to sleep outside or in the garage as punishment. Poor Lulu, I'm always thinking. I identify with Lulu – she's my old doll, her hair has been badly cut, she has koki scribbles on her arms and dirty marks on her face from countless plasters. Her limbs and head can be pulled off and put back again. She is a shadow figure, the culprit, the evil one, the bad, hard-hearted girl. She is feral and forgotten, deeply and impossibly loved, even though she is scarred and unfortunate-looking.

The Poet And The Woodcutter

By Colleen Higgs

The husband invited the younger man into his home, to build more shelves. He was a poet, the older man. He had small hands, rather like bear paws in a children's book, and nearly as hairy. He could lie on his couch and visualise the new shelves. He couldn't build them, or not easily and effortlessly. So in his generous position of power and largesse, he gave the younger man a job.

The younger man was down on his luck, between things, staying with his sister. He was tall, able-bodied, and had large, tanned, capable hands. He was dangerous because in spite of being down on his luck, he was tall, dark and handsome. He looked like the prince disguised as a woodcutter in a fairy story. He wore a black hat at a jaunty angle, he smoked cigarettes that he rolled up himself. Sometimes he drove by on his way to swim at the dam on his sister's motorcycle. Sometimes when he rode by he wasn't wearing a shirt.

So, he came to make shelves for the poet. The poet's wife made him cups of tea and tried to think of things to talk to him about. He didn't chat much but he smiled easily, and made her laugh with the odd throw-away comment.

The poet's wife was also a writer. Of course she couldn't read her work to the poet, he was a real writer, a serious writer, a poet. He needed silence and he needed to listen to difficult jazz music. He needed to read the work of other serious poets who lived in Germany, Turkey, Israel and Poland – not the ramblings of his own wife.

The poet's wife took to reading her work to the woodcutter; let's call him that, the tall, silent, tender-hearted woodcutter. He listened to her poems and stories and she could tell he found them moving from the way his eyes crinkled up softly as he listened.

The poet was often away on important business, giving readings, signing books, meeting with other famous writers in big cities here and abroad.

The poet's wife was often alone in the big house with the new shelves and the tin roof that rustled in the wind. Or she would have been if not for the woodcutter who came round sometimes for a cup of tea, or to listen to her reading. Some days he walked past instead of riding the bike. He stopped and asked her to go with him to the dam for a swim. One particularly hot summer's evening she went swimming with the woodcutter and decided that she would go and live with him in the forest and become a real writer herself. And so she did.

Face Creams

By Colleen Higgs

I use Nivea, L'Oreal, sometimes Body Shop
I can't bring myself to spend hundreds of rands on what?
I like to see them arrayed on the dressing-tables
and shelves of other women.

The bedroom is a little dark, a soft white duvet on the bed
cosmetics, perfumes, lotions, potions
a secret arsenal of sweet-smelling beauty
tempt me in.

If it's safe, I open a jar, scoop out a lick
onto my hand, smooth it in, feel the softness
seep into my cheek, like the loving touch
of mother, not mine, but the one in stories,
the one who wears an apron and has well-groomed hair,
who knows what takes out red wine stains
who can diagnose chickenpox or yellow fever

In fact one of my mother's chief skills was diagnosing
and treating ailments. If she or the world had been different
she would have made an excellent GP
instead of being a woman who likes to visit doctors
for pills, potions, shots, ops, scans and tests.

I shut the jar, twist it closed
Slink out of the other woman's room
and hope she won't notice that
I smell like her.

Where Do Broken Hearts Go?

By Betty Mukashema

Oh mother,
Mother, I can't hear you!
Where is happiness, where does true happiness lie?
You left me lamenting
Now I can't guess nor imagine
What I can use an empty heart-cup for!

Remember, you swore this to me.
If only I could find happiness
My true happiness!
How it grandly walked out that door.
But oh! I know some day, the war will end,
And I'll see it coming my way.
For without true happiness
My sweet love would have to be untrue!

A Tender Heart

By Betty Mukashema

How you run when I approach:
Up above the shelf
Whenever I come to perform above your head
You only hesitate to secrete yourself.

Most adventurous of all
How I wish I could determine
How you spend your hours of ease,
What a tender heart!

How delightful to suspect
All the places you have trekked:
North, south, west and east,
Will your expedition come to a halt?
What a tender heart!

Why be so shy?
My tender and lovely heart!
We are sisters, though I in your midst,
Appear darkness at noontime
What a tender heart!

Home To Die

By Winnie Munyarugerero

Mbabazi was a tall and athletic girl, a star in the school athletic team. Her school, Rutooma Full Primary School, deep in rural western Uganda, looked up to her to win the one hundred and two hundred metre races whenever schools of the area competed in athletics. In addition, Mbabazi, who loved to sing, was an active member of the school choir.

Thanks to the Universal Primary Education government programme, Mbabazi completed Primary Seven, but that marked the end of her educational journey. Not that she wanted it that way, or was a dull student. Far from it; she actually loved school and her performance was always above average. Unfortunately, her family was so poor that secondary school fees were way beyond what they could ever hope to afford.

After dropping out of school at the age of fifteen, Mbabazi became part of the village rhythm of planting and harvesting, digging and weeding, cooking and carrying. Only one thing broke the monotony and brought a smile to her face: the choir practice on Fridays and singing in the church choir on Sundays.

A girl in such a situation longs for marriage. When, therefore, on his annual leave, Muzora showed interest in her, Mbabazi was over the moon. Muzora, a holder of a Uganda Certificate of Education and working away in town, was, by all standards, a good catch. Better dressed than the village men, definitely with more money in his pocket, he had about him an aura of prosperity, confidence and modernity; a man that

55

had been to places and seen many faces, a man of the world. To Mbabazi, this was the Prince Charming come to lift her from the drudgery of village poverty.

The courtship was brief. Their villages being adjacent, the two young people were no strangers. True, Muzora was much older; Mbabazi had started primary school as he was finishing. But their families were distantly connected and visited occasionally. Therefore, by the time Muzora returned to town after his one-month leave, most of the marriage negotiations and requirements had been fulfilled. What remained was for him to go back to town to put together enough money for the wedding.

Four months were enough for him to make the required money. He returned to the village, and after the wedding, which was considered a huge success, the groom carried his beaming eighteen-year-old bride off to his one-roomed rented quarters in town.

Their first child, a boy, was born eleven months later. It soon became clear that with the added demands of the baby, Muzora's income as a junior clerk could not support the family in town. The young mother and baby Simon had to go back to the village where Mbabazi would grow food in the garden instead of buying it in the market. The long-legged, carefree girl who loved to run and to sing in the choir, returned as wife and mother, shouldering the responsibility of tilling the land, tending the family animals and taking care of her ailing parents-in-law. Truly, the honeymoon was over.

Muzora visited as often as was possible, and Mbabazi travelled to town whenever she could get away. But these visits got fewer and fewer as the two got busier and needed to save every bit of time and money to invest in Simon's education, and that of the other children to come. The two soon resigned themselves to an occasional weekend visit by the husband.

It was on one such visit that Mbabazi was struck with fear when she noticed how thin and sickly her husband looked. Later in bed, when she put her arms round him, she felt the bones sticking out at her. "You've lost a lot of weight, what's eating you up?" she asked.

"You're right. I haven't been well these last few months. I've been working too hard, I suppose. And with no one to cook at home, I don't get to eat proper meals."

"You should take better care of yourself. I hate to see you so thin," Mbabazi advised.

"It's nothing serious."

But to Mbabazi it was serious, only she couldn't voice her true fear. In the dark next to her husband she opened her mouth to ask if he had tested for HIV, but shut it again. That, she knew, was the one question men hated to be asked. Her women friends told how that was a question that earned slaps or kicks from their husbands. Mbabazi had long learnt that a husband, as father of the children, the salary-earner, was considered the supreme head of the family, the provider: not to be questioned. She sighed, which prompted her husband to ask, "What's the matter? What are you thinking about?"

"It's nothing."

In spite of her fear and anxiety about her husband's health, when he drew her to him, she responded. It didn't even occur to her to pull back, for in her world it was unheard-of for a wife to refuse the husband's desires. Why else, after all, did a girl leave her parents' home if not to warm her husband in bed whenever he wanted? Moreover, if truth be told, her own body was on fire for her man after months of involuntary abstinence. But even as the two bodies heaved in unison, at the back of her mind, fear remained.

Fear of what could be; fear because she was only too familiar with HIV/AIDS as were most people in her village, and for good reason. They had on several occasions received back their loved ones from towns in coffins or as the emaciated, prematurely-aged walking dead, brought home to die.

Mbabazi managed to push the fear away and enjoyed her husband's weekend stay. Muzora returned to town, and she went back to a work routine so heavy that she soon couldn't afford the luxury of worrying about the health of an absent husband. All the same it was with relief that she saw a healthy-looking Muzora on his next visit. The hollows in the cheeks had filled up, the sallow skin once again shone with life. He was his old happy self once again. All was well. There was nothing to fear, after all.

What shock, then, when only two months after Muzora's departure, Mbabazi got a message to hurry to town to nurse her critically ill husband! She found him in hospital in a coma from which he didn't recover. That same week, broken and confused, she returned home on a truck bearing her husband's body and belongings.

The burial over, mourners gone, the widow expected sympathy, support and understanding, all of which she got in good measure from those around, except the one person she most expected it from: her mother-in-law. The older woman brooded and sulked, hovering around like a cloud about to burst with rain. She shuffled about muttering and grumbling.

Fellow villagers shook their heads and said, "Poor woman! The death of her son has hit her hard."

Her brooding soon gave way to outbursts. At the slightest provocation she would roar and rant at her bewildered husband, at little Simon, or anybody else in sight, but most often at "that barren woman", Mbabazi. She abused her at every turn, shouting about how only Mbabazi could have killed her beloved son, how she had infected him with AIDS. According to her, Mbabazi's womb was shut by AIDS.

"Married for a whole six years and what's there to show for it? Only one child! I knew all along the woman was no good for my son. He would be alive today if he had listened to me and married Roza, Kagunga's daughter, whose wide hips and big behind gave promise of fertility," she cried out to anyone who cared to listen.

True, she had never received Mbabazi with open arms, but the two had learnt to get on with a degree of civility and politeness. This was no more. The abuse and taunts got worse by the day.

Mbabazi often wanted to answer back, but always stopped herself in time. The poor woman was hurting over her son's death, she reasoned. Moreover, no-one, including her own parents, would ever forgive her for exchanging words with the woman who gave birth to her husband, who was grandmother to her Simon. As long as her mother-in-law did not attack her physically, she decided she would bear the abuse. After all, as far as knew, words never killed anyone. She convinced herself that with time she would learn to ignore them.

But it hurt her deeply that her mother-in-law claimed that Mbabazi had killed her husband. It hurt so much so that instead of getting out of mourning, she sank deeper into depression and ill health. For if anybody was to be blamed, it was Muzora who not only got himself infected but also infected his wife and, possibly, their son as well. From the moment her mother-in-law mentioned AIDS, Mbabazi's body and mind accepted it as a fact that Muzora had died of the dreaded disease.

Certain that she was soon to follow her husband to the grave, she gave up any will to live, opening herself up to all manner of sickness. If it was not a headache today, it was fever the next, or a loose stomach the day after. She made no effort to get treatment, considering it a waste of time. She let her head hang down in misery and resignation.

Within only two months of her husband's death, Mbabazi's shoulders and head had drooped. A blank stare replaced the former sparkle in her eyes.

Meanwhile, her mother-in-law continued to abuse and harass her. One day, in a frenzy, with a pestle raised high above her head, the older woman hurled herself at Mbabazi. Were it not for her father-in-law, who was near enough to throw himself between the two women and wrench the pestle away from his wife, Mbabazi's head would have been smashed into pieces.

That was the last straw. Mbabazi mustered enough strength to gather up her belongings and pack them onto a boda boda. Clutching Simon on her lap, she boarded another boda boda and followed her luggage. They headed for her parents' home, never to return – so she told a neighbour before their departure.

"Let me go and die at home, away from this hatred," she said. At her home, her parents did all they could to nurse their daughter, but to no avail. She edged closer to death every passing day.

In desperation, Petero, Mbabazi's father, decided to do something. The sight of his once beautiful daughter reduced to a skeleton was too much to bear. He woke up earlier than usual one Saturday morning and announced to his wife, "I'm going to sell Kitanga in the market today. Pray that I get a good price."

Kitanga was the biggest of the six goats that comprised the entire family wealth. He dragged the bleating goat to Rutooma market, two kilometres away. Fortunately, his wife's prayers seemed to have worked, for he returned early in the afternoon, all smiles. He instructed his wife to get Mbabazi's things ready so he could take her to Mbarara Hospital the next day for treatment.

"To Mbarara! Where in Mbarara? Please don't take my daughter to die among strangers. Allow me to nurse her to the end," his wife pleaded.

"Stop the stupidity, woman! Who's talking of dying? Just do what I say. I'm taking my daughter to Mbarara tomorrow." The next day, Petero, with Mbabazi holding on to him, boarded a Morning Star coach to Mbarara town, some one hundred kilometres away. Mzee Petero had never been to Mbarara before and was a little apprehensive, but he was a man of faith and believed he would be able to find his nephew, Rwego, son to his sister. Rwego was a big man in the police force in Mbarara, and such a man would not be difficult to find. But if he failed to locate him, he at least had enough money for a return journey home.

Indeed it was easy to get to the police station and to the big Afande's house. Rwego was a kind and generous man. After listening to his uncle's account of the nature and origin of the disease as he understood it, Rwego knew where to take Mbabazi. And so they went to TASO for counselling and HIV testing.

The blood test was negative. Not convinced that she was AIDS-free, Mbabazi begged for a second test, just to make sure. Again the result was negative. Like the biblical paralytic whom Jesus told, "Get up, pick up your mat and walk", Mbabazi – who had been carried to TASO – left walking, laughing and throwing her arms in the air to praise God. She didn't care if people thought she was mad.

Her health returned so dramatically that by the time she returned to Rutooma village after a week, the whole village gaped in wonder. They couldn't believe their eyes.

Soon Mbabazi was once again the happy girl, singing in the church choir. However, she vowed never to marry again. Although she wasn't sure anymore that Muzora had died of AIDS, she would never again risk contracting the disease from any husband. Once bitten twice shy, she told herself.

But Mbabazi was not without challenge. Villagers smiled and whispered that only time would tell. 'Indeed, time will tell', Mbabazi responded to their smiles.

The Sacrifice

By Constance Obonyo

Joyce Nyaketcho moved slightly, fanning the flies that were gathering around her freshly smeared legs. The fresh banana leaf did just fine. "They are attracted to petroleum jelly," she explained to her best friend, Sheila Nyachwo.

"The flies disturb me too, after I have had a bath and smeared petroleum jelly on my body, but there is no choice now, is there?" The two girls laughed out loud.

"Joyce," Sheila said, her expression suddenly becoming serious, "I understand you are going to marry Mr Opendi. Is it true?"

Joyce lowered her eyes, embarrassed. "You heard right, Sheila. I promised my mother I would." She turned to her friend, imploring: "Mama says he is a rich man. He will look after me. I do not wish to be poor. He lives in a house with an iron roof and his children are all in school..." Joyce faltered on, seeing Sheila's worried expression.

"Joyce, he is over fifteen years older than you. What will you talk about? Besides, you are only a few years older than his eldest child. Have you thought about that?"

"Sheila," Joyce said thoughtfully, "I would like to live in a house with a concrete floor, with no dust in it. I do not ever want to worry about where my next meal will come from, let alone having to endure seeing my children without basic things like food or school fees. I would like to be respected in the village square – like other rich men's wives. Who in this village of Pajwenda does not respect Mama Brenda? My mother said my children would never lack for anything. I would like that. Jamie said I would not have to dig either… What is it?"

"Jamie? You are now down to first names? You have talked about this with Mr Opendi already? Joyce, this is not right! I am your best friend. The least you could have done was to run it by me first."

"Listen to me, Sheila," Joyce said urgently, grabbing Sheila's hand. "I have talked to him. He is a good man. I think he loves me. Maybe older than I am, but I think I can be happy with him. Besides, he is quite good-looking…"

"Joyce, I just want the best for you. Please, do not make rash decisions. Think about it for at least three months or so. Just be careful," Sheila implored.

The two girls were standing now, no longer sitting on the small verandah of Joyce's family's rectangular main hut. The beautiful neat ochre designs on the walls meant nothing to Joyce anymore. She dreamt of living in a brick house with an iron-sheet roof. Wealth was beckoning her; and she was not going to shy away from it – never!

Mama Joyce came from the well, balancing her pot delicately on her banana-leaf-cushioned head.

"Eh, Mama! You should not be doing that at your age; Joyce should be doing that for you. Here, let me help you," said Sheila as she reached out to help Mama Joyce lower the huge pot of water from her head.

"I cannot let Joyce do that. She is soon to be a bride, you know. Has she not told you?" she looked at the girls questioningly.

"Oh yes she has," said Sheila. "I had better be on my

way. Mama must be looking for me by now." Sheila turned abruptly and set off towards the other end of the path Mama Joyce had just come by.

"What is up with her?" Mama Joyce asked her daughter, concern starting to crowd her otherwise flawless face. Even at her age, she was still a beautiful woman.

"Do not worry about her, Mama, she is just upset about Jamie. She thinks he is too old for me. And because his children are about my age, she thinks that could be a problem," replied Joyce.

"My daughter, nothing in this world comes smooth. You just have to take it in your stride. Granted, he may be too old for you, but as I have already said, he is rich. Besides, those children will be grown up and out of there in no time, and then you will have the home all to yourselves and your children. It is just a matter of time, my dear. You must be patient. Many of the village women have started envying me already."

Just then Joyce's youngest brother, Owori, ran towards them. He was in tears and quite out of breath. "You are my worst nightmare!" he blurted out, pointing at Joyce. "Ogolla does not want to talk to me anymore. He says you are going to marry his father! Oh, I am so embarrassed. It is all over school!"

Joyce stared at him, speechless. Mama Joyce grabbed Owori and started beating him. She was furious. "How can you berate your sister so? She is the envy of every girl and mother in this village! I do not ever want to hear you disrespect her this way, do you understand?" she bellowed, lifting a frightened Owori from the ground to her fuming face.

Owori stopped crying. His anger gave way to deep fear. He had never seen his mother so agitated. She had never lifted a finger to attack anybody before, let alone beat them.

Owori had not realised that this thing about the marriage between Joyce and that man Opendi was sacred to his mother. He was confused. Did she not know that the man had children, one of them his own age? Didn't she care? What about his father; what did he make of it? Were his parents going to give away his sister to an old man because he lived in a brick house with an iron-sheet roof? What was the world coming to?

The small village of Pajwenda was soon abuzz with the news of James Opendi's beautiful soon-to-be wife and their upcoming wedding.

Mr Opendi's late wife, Stella, had perished in a nasty road accident at the notorious Lugazi black spot on the Tororo-Malaba highway. The whole village had seemed to come to a standstill, for Stella had been highly regarded. She had been the chair of the Mother's Union of the local Anglican Church, handling many of the church's activities, especially those to do with widows and orphans and their welfare.

It had been only a few months since Stella's death, but her husband already seemed to have forgotten her. Although this raised eyebrows, it was one of those things that was never discussed in public. Even so, there had been whispers about the way Mr Opendi had handled his grief – or was it the lack of it? There were some in the village who looked forward to the festivities because they meant a lot of merrymaking and eating. They certainly looked forward to eating a lot of meat, because most of them were poor people, and only got to eat meat on important days like Christmas. Mr Opendi was a rich man and there was bound to be a lot of meat at the wedding.

Many of the village girls and their mothers were green with envy, because Mama Joyce's daughter would get to live in a brick house with an iron-sheet roof. She would soon become a little madam in the village, and at such a young age too!

The wedding was a success. Mr Opendi did not disappoint the village paupers; there was a lot of meat to eat, so much that the villagers could carry some home for their children's breakfast the following day.

Sheila was Joyce's maid of honour, even though she was not married. That was a requirement the local church waived, for Joyce had put her little (and soon-to-be) rich foot down over the matter, and would not budge.

Joyce went away to live happily ever after in Mr Opendi's cherished brick-walled, iron-roofed house with his five children. Or so she thought.

The 'fairytale' marriage first started showing cracks when Mr Opendi's relatives accused Joyce of bewitching their brother. They said he had started ignoring them the day he married Joyce. They told Mr Opendi's children not to respect her because she was a witch.

"Witch!" the neighbourhood children would shout at Joyce whenever they saw her pass by from the well with her pot of water.

"I understand she did something to him. He no longer helps any of his relatives financially," the villagers whispered whenever she passed by.

Mr Opendi's relatives dispatched several delegations to talk to him about his wife's supposed witchcraft. His children were enlisted as well.

"Just ignore them, my darling," Mama Joyce said when Joyce went to her with her concerns. "They are just jealous."

One day, Ogolla, Mr Opendi's youngest son, fell ill. Try as she might to treat him, he refused to take his anti-malarial tablets, fearing that Joyce might bewitch him. Mr Opendi was not at home at the time. He had gone to Kampala to purchase stock for his retail shop at Pajwenda trading centre.

One of the children decided to go to the next village, Mulanda, to call one of their relatives, Aunt Apio, to attend to young Ogolla. Unfortunately, by the time he returned with Aunt Apio, Ogolla was shivering all over. He soon went into a coma, and was rushed to a nearby health centre on a bicycle, only to be pronounced dead on arrival.

Aunt Apio ran along the road all the way from the health centre at Mulanda to Pajwenda village, wailing and calling Joyce names. "The witch, the witch, she has started her work, she has started what she came to do, Ogolla is dead!"

On hearing her wails, the villagers gathered on the roads and followed her. By the time they reached Pajwenda, some of them did not even know why they were in the crowd. They were all shouting, "Down with her, down with the witch! She must not continue, we must not let her continue!"

The crowd got to Mr Opendi's compound and found Joyce threshing millet for the family, whereupon they descended upon her and tore her to pieces. Within minutes, Joyce's mutilated bleeding body lay on the bare dirt compound. The crowd then proceeded to the family garden, where they destroyed all their crops, even cutting down the banana plantation.

Mr Opendi met them at Pajwenda trading centre as he was returning home. They were crazed and beady-eyed, chanting, "Witch, witch, she was a witch..."

Then they melted away, each returning to their homes on the way to Mulanda.

The Cabinet Minister

By Constance Obonyo

The Cabinet Minister
Has snatched
My wife!
The distraught
Shrieks
Of the Civil Servant
Rend the air

He must go!
Cries the crowd

Let him
Without a plank
In eye
Step forth
And fish
The mote
In mine!
Bellows
The Cabinet Minister

The crowd
Is silent!
Among them
Are Scribes

Sadducees
Elders
Chief Priests
And Teachers
Of the Law
The rest
Are Pharisees

The Cabinet Minister
Has snatched
My wife!
The moans
Of the Civil Servant
infiltrate the air
The crowd
Is silent,
Dead silent!

Until I Find Salama

By Mastidia K. Mbeo

It was almost 10 o'clock at night, when Salama's father, Mr. Mkali picked a quarrel with his wife, Nyamwiza. Nyamwiza was preparing bites for family breakfast.

"Where is Salama?" Mkali asked his wife.

"She...she is celebrating her 18th birthday at a nearby hall." Nyamwiza replied.

"What! Celebrating at night? Is she a prostitute?" Mkali said furiously. And Nyamwiza was stunned but she tried to keep cool.

"No... but...but she told me that she asked for permission from you and you even contributed some money for buying drinks. I knew you were aware of everything! She replied.

"It doesn't matter whether I have made the contribution or not. What matters is that she is not here at such a time of the night. What I want is to maintain discipline in my house. Can you imagine, such a young girl, a child, staying outside at such an hour? I cannot tolerate such behaviour. And you, woman, I know that you know everything about your daughter, but you are keeping secrets.

"Now, I don't want to hear anybody opening my door for her. If you do so, I will chase both of you away. And yes, I' serious. I will do anything for the sake of my daughter." Nyamwiza smiled inwardly and wondered how sending her and her daughter out of the house was meant to protect the daughter. But she did not say anything to Mkali.

71

"Do you really think I would be happy to see our daughter spoilt?" She asked her husband.

"I am only saying that what I want is discipline, tell your daughter to behave herself." Mkali insisted.

Nyamwiza was offended by her husband's attitude. Whenever there was a bad case with Salama, she became Nyamwiza's daughter and whenever she excelled at anything, she was Mkali's daughter. This time she did not want to own up to Mkali's attitude. But she knew she had to do something. The night was getting darker and darker and the Salama was not coming. Nyamwiza was getting very worried. 'May be she has met with some problems on the way back,' she thought. One idea after another floated in her mind and she kept quiet for some time, wondering what to do. Then she decided to follow Salama at the hall. She had to find her daughter.

Nyamwiza left the house carefully without letting her husband know that she was moving out. She left the door unbolted so that she could return with Salama unnoticed. When she dashed into the dark night, her mind got crowded with thoughts of fear and uncertainty. 'Suppose...suppose... suppose', her heart pounded, but she walked on anyway and murmured a short prayer to God.

Nyamwiza proceeded into darkness. She passed several houses and did not meet any one. But as she turned round a corner leading to the village dispensary, she saw a tall figure walking towards her. Then she noticed it was a man. He was tall and gigantic.

Nyamwiza's heart somersaulted several times. She could not turn back and she could not run. Either way, she felt trapped. Then she decided to brave it and started balancing alternatives in her head. 'I will bite him if he dares to touch me. I will scream and call residents to lynch him if he dares to lay his fingers on me. I will run and run if he turns out to be dangerous. I will... I will... I will...

In the meantime, the man was drawing nearer, closing the distance between them. Suddenly they were face to face. Nyamwiza's heart pounded faster and without thinking she blurted out a greeting.

"Good evening sir." The man did not answer. Nyamwiza thought of running ahead but for a while her legs could not move.

A few steps away, her legs felt better and she started walking very fast. When she stole a glance backwards, she realised that the man was following her. He too was walking very fast! Nyamwiza got very scared and her mind went straight to rape! She had heard of many rape cases in her village especially at night. She prayed to God not to let that happen to her. She then broke into a run and when she looked back again, the man was running after her.

"My God"! She shouted as she sprinted forward.

By God's grace, Nyamwiza was a stone throw from one of the houses in the village and some people were sitting outside the house, chatting and laughing. Nyamwiza stormed into their compound. When she looked back, the man was still following her. Nyamwiza could not wait. She sprinted past the laughing crowd outside the house and got into the house where she fell right into another man's arms.

"Who are you and where are you going?" he asked her. Nyamwiza did not answer. She just stared at him and pointed at the man following her. The men outside accosted him and one of them asked him what he wanted. Like a mad person he was jumping up and down shouting!

"I want that woman, who has entered this compound! I want that woman! She is my friend! A long time friend! We have been together for the whole day, drinking and chatting, but now she is trying to escape from me. Tell her to come out otherwise you are going to regret. She has to pay for my things!"

Nyamwiza was now hiding in one of the rooms inside the house but she could clearly hear him. Trembling, she thought about her marriage and about how the stupid man could easily make her lose her dignity before her family and the community.

"By the way, who is she?" One of the men outside was asking. "You never know, may be it is true that she has failed to keep her promises."

A smaller voice interrupted the man asking and it was a woman's voice. "She is behind the house," the woman said. "Run after her before darkness swallows her. She pointed him to another direction. The man who must have been drunk did not wait to ask. He just took off like lightening, heading behind the house.

Nyamwiza did not hesitate. She too stormed out of the house again and run for dear life. She ran till she reached her home. Like a thief, she entered the house and quickly fastened the door behind her. Her husband was already snoring in deep slumber.

It was after she slumped into a chair in her living room that she remembered what her mission had been; to find her daughter.

Nyamwiza was roused from her shock by a sudden knock at the door. Before she knew what she was doing, she was next to the bed, vigorously shaking her husband and telling him that a man was following her.

"Where is he?"

"Outside."

"But why do you say that he is following you?"

"Because I saw him."

"Women and their cowardly nature! How can he be following you when you are inside the house and he is outside?"

Remembering how she had left the house in the first place, Nyamwiza just shut up and crouched behind her husband as he opened the door.

When the door finally opened, Salama walked in. Her white teeth and eyes sparkled with excitement.

"It was a great party. Thank you dad! Thank you Ma!" Nyamwiza and Mkali turned at the same time and stared at each other in disbelief as Salama delivered her appreciation.

The Drinking Jar

By Philomena Nabweru Rwabukuku

She balanced the pot on her head, her neck graceful as a giraffe's, as she glided down the path, quickly covering the space between the village well and her homestead. As she walked the familiar path, she gloried in the luxurious green of sprouting, flowering crops of beans, groundnuts, cabbage, peas and pumpkin that had little droplets of water shining silver in the early morning sun.

She cast a quick glance at the suckers that would soon stand heavy with bunches of plantain, and felt a glow spread through her body to warm her feet numbed by the dew. The field of millet and that of sorghum were on her right. She paused to inhale the rich scent that always wafted from the ripening millet. She savoured it for a while and continued homeward to unburden herself of the heavy water pot on her head. She was Nyonza, Nyamwezi's wife.

Nyamwezi was a well-respected elder, just as his wife was. He was very wealthy and all envied him his good fortune. His household was big, with a lot of men and women who were at his beck and call. There was indeed a lot of work for them, as there were kraals and kraals of cattle, as well as pens full of goats and sheep. The chickens were uncountable. He was the only farmer in all the land around who reared rare birds such as geese, ducks and guinea fowls. His fields and plantations were extensive, covering hills and valleys. All sorts of crops were grown: coffee, cotton, vegetables, cereals and tubers.

77

Nyamwezi sat on the veranda of his hut as he had always done since the time he married Nyonza. It had now become a ritual that started his days. Every morning he looked forward to her return from the well. As far as he could remember, he had never seen her support her pot with her hands, and yet she had never dropped it. That same pot his mother had given to her when, as a bride, she had gone to the well for the first time. He had eagerly waited for her then. How she had shone brighter than the dawn, how his heart had sung at the sight! She still moved as effortlessly as she had done then, his goddess, his priestess, who administered to him body and soul.

Thoughts of these early days soon had him remembering his younger days, when he had had several wives and many children, all of whom had perished during the great famine so many years ago. Ha, that great famine where even mothers would hide the meagre food from their own offspring, and husbands would threaten to wring their wives' necks if they did not tell them where they had hidden what little food there was! Some had even gone beyond these threats and done worse...

He paused as he stared blankly recalling those very painful years of despair and loss. He drew in a slow breath and remained silent with his head bent towards his vast chest, looking like a bull sitting on its haunches: a great bull that rules the kraal. He was a sad bull. This bull sighed deeply, and his hands moved listlessly.

The only survivor of that household was Nyonza, his first wife, who, he sadly realised, was almost past child-bearing age. The lady was so kind-hearted to all the young that many wished she were their mother. They often found excuses to stray into her hut for a motherly hug or a bite of something. She would take time off to talk to whichever young person came to her. She would offer them groundnut paste, roasted groundnuts, simsim or corn. All those who visited the Nyamwezis praised their generosity and wished God had made them a happier couple by making them parents.

"What is a lot of wealth for if you have no child to call your own?" they would ask.

Despite their age, both husband and wife still hoped and prayed that God in his goodness would soon remember them. Years came and went, and God did not seem to hear their prayers.

When almost all hope was gone, Nyonza had a dream. In her dream, she saw an old woman who had come to visit her late in the evening. The old woman was dressed in rags and leaned heavily on a walking stick. She was old, old, old. Nyonza woke at the point in her dream where she was eagerly welcoming the old lady, about to help her sit on a clean mat she had just spread out in her hut. At the same time, the old woman was beginning to say something to her when a noise startled Nyonza awake.

She soon realised it was the Shepard's dog barking. Since that night she had known no peace as she had that dream over and over again, making it difficult for her to decide what was dream and what was truth or fact.

For months, Nyonza thought about nothing else but her dream. She searched gatherings, wedding parties, marketplaces and funerals, but did not see any old woman who resembled the one she had seen in her dream. Many times Nyonza followed various old women, only to reach them and realise they were not her Old One, as she had come to call the old lady in her mind. Desperately she visited all the old women in the nearby villages. Twice she journeyed to the villages where her mother's sisters had migrated. She saw no old woman such as the one she sought.

And the dreams intensified with each passing day until they became second nature. Eventually, she was no longer sure of her sanity. The few nights she fell sound asleep, she would see the old woman at the beginning of the dream but whenever she woke up, she would not be sure whether the Old One was an old man or woman. And the old woman or old man would have been in bed with her doing all sorts of erotic things with her!

Nyamwezi noticed his wife's restlessness immediately and wondered what was bothering her. He had long stopped expressing his unhappiness about their childlessness. Everything else was in order. He knew that he loved her without any reservations and that she too knew it; he did his best to show her love, care, respect, everything. And since Nyonza was not complaining, he could not help feeling at a loss.

When months elapsed, and Nyonza no longer slept at night, nor did much work in the fields, nor ate proper meals, Nyamwezi decided to confront her. He had to know what was on her mind to have changed her so. Was she contemplating suicide, was she… was Nyonza… eeeeh! What was it that ailed her?

"Nyonza, my dear wife, the one with whom we have undergone all hardships, tell me, my good one. What it is that troubles you?"

Nyonza did not share her dreams with her husband because she could not explain even to herself why she was so obsessed with the idea of an old woman visiting her; moreover,

one she had only seen in a dream. Deep down inside her, however, she felt that the old woman (or was it an old man?), would be good for her. In some subtle way, she knew that the Old One in her dreams had something important to tell her.
So in order to show her appreciation for her husband's concern, she vaguely explained her moods and then, much more carefully, she continued her search for the Old One.

Nyamwezi in turn kept watch over her, afraid of losing her to whatever it was that was slowly eating her up. He even started following her, vaguely suspicious that perhaps she was going to meet someone else – a man? Her lack of interest in any intimacy intensified this feeling.

"My love, will you let me hold or touch you?" he would plead.

His wife did not say much, but he could tell that she no longer wanted him in that way. She even kept their bodies from touching. And yet whenever she fell asleep, all these inhibitions disappeared as she came to him, cuddling, caressing, with erotic movements he had never known from her before. But alas, as soon as he reciprocated, she would withdraw like a tortoise into its shell. In all this anguish, he needed explanations. Where was she getting these new tactics from? And why, why would she no longer allow him to touch her, love her? Perhaps his suspicions were valid? Days turned into weeks and weeks to months; nine whole months and that haunted look in Nyonza became intensified by her loss of weight and listlessness. Nyamwezi searched his mind for any wrong phrase he might have uttered. He remembered his points of weakness: although his heart had not been in it, several times he had told her that he would take another wife to get children. Resigned silence had been her only response. There were also times when memories of the past overwhelmed him, making him lose his usually well-managed temper. Otherwise he could not explain what was amiss.

He recalled all the sweet moments when they had wooed and loved. He dreamt of their first few months together, wishing to rewind the clock if only to see that endearing smile again, and hear that lilting laugh that still sent his heart banging against his ribcage.

Nyonza was still the most lovely woman he had ever known. The passing years had done nothing to alter her comeliness. Her eyes were light and clear, making one think of early morning sunshine. Somehow he always thought of her as light or flowers, white and pure. The years with her had enhanced rather than diminished this feeling. Nyonza, whose voice had first captured his heart, still made his skin tingle with pleasurable surprise. When she spoke, her voice made him think of music, of little bells tinkling, or the nanga playing. She still moved as gracefully as a gazelle, her shapeliness making the heads of both men and women turn. She was a crested crane whose crown of hair was soft as kapok, with numerous curls like those found on babies' heads.

His Nyonza, whom God had spent much valuable time moulding, had given him much pleasure and peace. These and many other thoughts stole Nyamwezi's sleep, forcing him to hear and feel his wife's struggles as she turned, fretted and murmured in her restlessness. For many weeks he had resisted touching her because he realised that she slept so little, so lightly. Besides, he wanted to love an awake, conscious Nyonza so that he could know if she still truly loved and desired him.

Meanwhile a storm slowly gathered strength. The wind

blew and howled. Frightened birds sought refugee in their nests. The neighbours called to each other in their hurry not to be caught in the rain. The herdsmen hurriedly drove the livestock by as thunderbolt followed thunderbolt. Lightning threatened everything in its path and the shepard dog howled and barked, running among the animals, its bell ringing "clang, cling, clang" as if to warn them of imminent danger.

Nyonza glanced towards the veranda where Nyamwezi stood motionless, clearly flinching at each bang and echo of the thunder, heightening her sense of anxiety. She knew just how patient he had been with her, not pressing for explanations, intimate contact or conversation. In a detached way, she imagined what her husband might be thinking or feeling, but she did not dwell on it. She was very preoccupied with her Old One, and what all this might portend for the future. Nyamwezi did not seem to fit in it anymore. "The Old One and I, I wonder where this madness will end," she mused.

*****

Nyonza deftly gathered the foodstuffs which had been spread out in the sun, putting them in their respective granaries, completing this task just before the first fat drops of rain landed. They were lazy raindrops, following each other reluctantly. Nyonza half-smiled at the thought of the rain being slow at running or walking, like a man or woman who took forever to complete tasks. The rain sometimes promised to fall, but failed.

She dwelt on this idea a bit longer, even reviewing her childhood preoccupation with who made rain, where it came from, whether there was a huge never-drying reservoir up in the sky, or if God ever cried from his one, huge all-seeing eye! Then all of a sudden, feeling weary, she straightened up and sighed aloud. "If only I had at least one wee, little child, to eat some of this food! Now why do I work? For whom do I toil?" She went on murmuring to herself in misery.

As the raindrops began to hurtle down, she heard an unusual sound. She listened intently. What was it she was hearing? It was clearer now. She heard the approach of one who was tired, whose steps seemed to drag and falter, who stopped and started again. Would the rain wait for her before it started coming down in sheets?

Was she hallucinating? She pinched herself to check, shook herself and found that she was not asleep. The old woman who was approaching had her eyes fixed on the ground close to her walking stick.

As she drew nearer, Nyonza saw that she was dressed in rags. Clean rags of all colours were arranged to cover every part of her body except the feet, eyes and hands. Her left hand held a small, shining, brown, drinking gourd. She moved ever so slowly, and yet seemed to be getting close quickly. Her height, though diminished by age, was still discernable.

When she was close, she paused and said, "Beautiful daughter, don't you know how to welcome the tired ones?" Her deep husky voice drew Nyonza from her stupor, and she began fussing over the old woman. She was so taken up with making the old lady comfortable that it took her a while to notice that the rain was now falling in torrents.

"Mother, people are always welcome to my house, especially old ones like you. Mother, I am blessed to have you come to my little house. I have never been this delighted to have a visitor, oh Mother, oh Old One!"

She carefully helped the old woman sit on a newly woven mat, a mat she had not allowed anyone else to sit on. This mat had colours that commanded eyes to look at it. It made one think of the rainbow that holds the rain, removes the power of the sun's heat and yet lights up the hills and the valleys.

Despite the heavy clouds outside, this mat also seemed to light up the whole room. Nyonza went down on her knees before the old lady and held out both hands in greeting. The old lady looked Nyonza in the eyes without saying a word. Her eyes were questioning and searching. When she took Nyonza's hands, the surprisingly soft fingers firmly gripped her elbows.

A sweet, wrinkled smile hovered on her lips, lighting up the old face, making it look young and happy. A warm comfortable feeling enveloped Nyonza, making her relive the times her mother used to hug her. She wished this Old One would never let go. But she had to serve her something.

Nyonza carefully disengaged herself and moved quickly into an inner room. She brought out the beautifully woven basket in which she kept the roasted coffee beans sweetened with honey that many a good wife served visitors to make them especially welcome. She fetched fresh milk treated with special herbs that gave it a rare aroma, knowing that an old lady of that age must cherish such a flavour. All this she offered to the old lady, who shook her head.

Nyonza then brought out fermented porridge, rich with the aroma of millet and sorghum, but still the old lady would not take it. At a loss, Nyonza stopped, briefly puzzled. Then slowly, a half-smile on her lips, she went and knelt before the

Old One, who spread out her arms and enfolded Nyonza in a tight, peaceful embrace. The rags had a faint scent that reminded Nyonza of the earthy aroma that rises from the thirsty ground when touched by the first drops of rain. Nyonza breathed in the rare perfume, and again the Old One searched her eyes.

When she eventually released her, there was an alluring smile that made the old face shine and Nyonza feel light, so light, as if a huge bundle of firewood had been lifted off her shoulders. She sighed deeply, wondering where all the happiness that now overwhelmed her was coming from.

The Old One still had to be offered something. Without hesitating, she got up in one fluid movement, went to the bedroom, and brought out a long-necked, beautifully decorated earthenware jar that contained Nyamwezi's favourite drink, a drink that Nyonza had learnt to brew from her mother.

On the eve of her wedding, she had been instructed in how careful she had to be while making the bushera, and what she had to do to keep it from going stale.

"My daughter," her mother had told her, handing her the jar, "now that you are getting married, you must always brew and keep this jar full of your dear one's favourite drink. Never allow it to dry up, nor allow anyone else, man or woman, ever to drink from it. And listen carefully, my child. This shall be your love potion, your gourdful of love." Nyonza had listened to her mother and had adhered to her advice to the letter.

"This drink is made from millet, sorghum and honey as you already know, my dear," her mother had continued. "For it to taste perfect, it takes careful cleaning of both the millet and sorghum. Using the winnowing tray (orugali), woven with shavings from the papyrus or similar reeds found in the marshes, the millet and sorghum are sifted to separate the grain from the stones, soil and chuff. The clean millet grain is then ground into a fine powder on a grinding stone. No roasting is required.

"After cleaning the sorghum, it is rubbed with ashes from the heart of the cooking place and then soaked in clean water and covered to keep out the light. Within three days, the sorghum sprouts and gets fermented. It is then spread out in the sun to dry, after which it is ground. Water is boiled. Millet flour is first stirred into clean drinking water and then the boiling water is poured onto the paste already made. Vigorous stirring must follow to ensure that the mixture forms no lumps, which will spoil good porridge. The fermented sorghum acts as yeast as it's stirred into the cooling porridge, breaking the thickness. Honey adds sweetness, flavour and quality.

"Given a day or two, depending on the individual taste, the brew will be ready to drink. Earthenware vessels or gourds keep such a drink cool and preserve the original taste and aroma. Bride, daughter mine, I am telling you all this not because you don't know, but because a mother must always say goodbye to the beautiful one, to prepare her for the long journey."

It was such a drink that Nyonza now thought of giving to the Old One. She had never violated the norm her mother had admonished her to observe. But today she felt she had to offer this old lady something, even if it meant betraying the honour and respect accorded her husband.

His image flitted through her mind, and she thought of how she had never known nor desired to be with any man except him. She felt dazed and fascinated by the thought of how he would react if he found this old lady thirstily drinking the brew that had exclusively been his, directly from his own jar! But was the Old One a man or a woman?

Nyonza watched, unable to tear her eyes away from the Old One's throat, which moved rapidly up and down, up and down, up and down. It was spellbinding! The Old One did not pause; she seemed to have stopped breathing, all her frail energies focused on the jar and the drink she was partaking of. The word intensity bounced through Nyonza's mind as she watched with uttermost attention.

As the Old One threw her head back to empty Nyamwezi's jar of his favourite drink, an unbearably warm feeling enveloped Nyonza. It was taking away all her breath, making her gasp. So hot, so warm, and yet so, so cool! So peaceful and yet so disturbing! Thoroughly overwhelmed with inexplicable ecstasy, Nyonza slowly came awake. She tried to move, but couldn't. Something held her very tightly. Very reluctantly she opened her eyes to find herself in the most rewarding embrace she had ever known from Nyamwezi.

The Goddess Of The Hills

By Margaret Ntakalimaze

Beyond the green hills of Kabale, close to the Rwandan border, a caravan proceeds towards Katuna. Soldiers armed with spears and shields, bows and arrows, guard the procession. There is tension in the air. A blanket shrouds a sky empty of birds. It is windy and the breeze chills the nerves. Everything is quiet, except for the sound of footsteps gathering speed.

Among the soldiers is a dark-skinned woman with beads around her waist, wrists and ankles. A leopard skin, the symbol of wealth and power, is wrapped tightly around her body. She walks majestically, waving a fly whisk. Her eyes are bloodshot and her mouth twitches with suppressed rage.

At dawn, when the caravan reaches its destination, horns are blown and drums are beaten to herald the arrival of the goddess of the hills. The whole village trembles as if lightning is about to strike.

"Nyabingi, the goddess of the hills is here. The owner of everything has arrived. Wake up! Wake up! Come one and all. She has come to cure us and bless us with plenty," a voice calls.

Everyone wakes up and welcomes her. Women, with children on their backs, dance and giggle. They clap their hands, while men select goats and cows for the huge offering that is to come. For many, it is a time of happiness.

As followers surround the dark-skinned woman, joy and laughter fill the air. The time has come to wash sins away by dipping hands in animal blood poured into a wide, black-and-white dotted calabash. This is a day of victory; victory from hunger and poverty. A day for barren women to conceive, for the sick to be healed, the lame to walk: all through Nyabingi's conquering spirit.

Suddenly, the goddess of the hills speaks through the dark-skinned woman. She speaks with authority. Her eyes brighten, she spins around, possessed by the spirit of the goddess of the hills. In a deep, haughty voice she addresses the gathering.

"Hmmm... hmmm... My people! My people! Worship me! Bow down and kneel before me, and I shall pour my blessings not only on you, but on your children and their children's children. I am the owner of everything on earth and you will lack for nothing. Just ask and you will receive."

The dark-skinned woman spins once again, and then, with her eyes focused on another world, she shouts, "People of my land, I am satisfied with what you have given me. Let this be a warning to you. Anyone who disobeys me will die a terrible death, and so will their children and great-grandchildren. Indeed, their whole clan will perish. But those who worship me will enjoy everything I possess: this land and its animals. For I am Nyabingi, goddess of the hills."

Still in a trance, the woman continues speaking, "My people, my people, I am angry with you. Some of you have left me to follow men with skin the colour of newborn babies. They tell you of a man who died long ago. How can a dead man, a man they have never seen, be a saviour, when I am here, alive, talking to you? Worship me, and the whole world will be yours."

When these words are uttered, there is a shift in the gathered crowd. Some of the people start trembling and others fall down. Foaming at the mouth, they scream and shout in terror. Some of them bite their tongues, while others try to speak in vain. Once again, the Nyabingi spirit is at war defending the goddess of the hills.

A distance away, some people hide their eyes from the dark-skinned woman. They ask questions but receive no answers.

<u>You Are The One</u>

By Margaret Ntakalimaze

The one I love says this
And I hear that
Lucky is the man
Who has the first love
Of a woman

Lucky is the woman
Who has the last love
Of a man

Remember this!
The matters of the heart
Are just about happiness

And you are the one
The only one
I love.

The Prodigal Son

By Olivia Jembere

With an expression that suggested meditation, the sixty-five-year-old Tichaona sat on a stone terrace. Some of the old people were scattered in groups, talking softly in low tones that did not reach him; others were walking around the courtyard of the New Hope old people's home. Tichaona lowered his head, his left hand covering his face as various scenes played over and over in his mind. He tried to shut out the images, but could not. He relived those moments time and again… "You killed him! You killed him! You bitch!"

Tichaona covered his eyes and pressed his fingers into the sockets until the pain drove out the images, but after a while, he saw his mother again. "I swear it on your life and the nine months I carried you!" The voice rang in his skull until a light touch on his shoulders pulled him back to the present.

"Are you okay?" asked Rufaro softly. She was one of the younger nurses who worked at the old people's home. Though she was well past twenty-four, she was still very beautiful. She was anxious that the nightmares that Tichaona was having were far from over. So many times he took long walks, and he was unusually reserved.

Rufaro heard all the words clearly but they didn't make sense. "So the nightmare had to do with what happened in your life?" He nodded.

"Sometimes I am scared of the darkness, afraid of falling asleep, afraid that if I open my eyes or close them, I might see that same shadow that haunts me."

Rufaro stared at him. "Whose shadow do you see?"

"My mother's. – dead these three decades now," he said.

"You know, when you're young, you think that you have a lot of years to live, that you have your life in your own hands: finishing school, acquiring wealth, getting married to a beautiful woman, having children and grandchildren," he paused. "But when you reach my age, you realise the importance of being at peace with every fellow human being – and our culture."

"Whatever happened, why don't you let it go now? You're a prisoner of your own thoughts," said Rufaro gently. He looked at her for a moment, a frown creasing his forehead. "You don't understand – there is no running away. What can't be cured must be endured. I've been cursed as a prodigal son." Rufaro felt like a woman deaf from birth, who had fleetingly been shown the miracle of hearing, and had an urge to hear more. "But why?" she questioned.

"Because of what I did. I felt I had no choice, but it was wrong. It took me so long to realise that my act was irrevocable." He sighed. "That unfortunate moment was destined to have a far-reaching effect on my future."

The pain came back fresh and strong, as he thought back to his childhood. It had happened so many years ago, and yet every instant of what had happened was still as clear in his mind as if it had taken place that day. "When I look back, I suppose everything started to go wrong after that moment." He shook his head. "It was against my puritanical upbringing."

His mind spun back to the late 1950s. There was the familiar green vista, a narrow valley where St Theresa's Mission was situated, with low-lying fields of maize and nodding yellow sunflowers, a languid river that wriggled through the mission, some clusters of huts and houses around a blue church, which had a huge cross. Faintly from across the river, the sounds of the mission could be heard: herd-boys flourishing their whips above flocks of lazily chewing cattle and goats, dogs barking, ululations, children calling, woman buzzing with conversation as they carried firewood, and an occasional clear laugh.

Opposite the church was the preacher's house. A small white house with a small garden in front, a dark wooden chicken-house on one side, and beyond it, a wavy field of green sugarcane. The home possessed a benign and friendly atmosphere.

Edward Tazvitya, the preacher (better known as Mufundisi Tazvitya) was in his late thirties, tall, dark and fiercely handsome. He was a kind, cheerful, sensitive man, and he played his role as a father to the community very well. The church was the pillar of his existence. After he had lost his parents at the age of four, Father Bob, a Swiss missionary, had taken him into the mission's orphanage, where he was raised. Edward valued his devout upbringing at St Anne's mission and this imbued him with delight in doing God's work.

Edward was blessed with a beautiful family that drew the admiration of the community. His wife, Ratidzo Tazvitya, was in her late twenties, very light in complexion. Their marriage was an unusual combination of endearing friendship, bubbly personalities and ready laughter. Ratidzo followed Edward around like a faithful dog when he made his occasional visits to the elderly, the sick or the bereaved, although she did not have her husband's ability to invite confidences; they knew he was capable of handling their issues. These mission folk were his people and he understood them.

Tichaona was the eldest child, in his early teenage years, good-looking and athletic. He had inherited nothing from his parents except his mother's complexion. He doted on his father and tried to ape him. This was no use, however, because he was naturally touchy, especially when he thought he was being unfairly treated. His mother knew the secret of his personality, and where his rebellious nature came from. She had stoically borne the nagging guilt that arose in her whenever she thought about her past.

Rutendo, twelve, and Ropafadzo, ten, had inherited their father's dark good looks and were so alike that one could easily have mistaken them for twins.

Tichaona was not close to his mother, and this was because of her insane jealousy over her friendship with Nomsa. Nomsa Juru was twelve, tall and lovely, with long dark hair that was always plaited. His relationship with Nomsa was more like "puppy love", and the mission had cosy places for secret meetings. The pair shared a lot – good times and bad, although it had not been that way from the beginning. At first, Tichaona didn't take much notice of Nomsa. However, during one Sunday service, when she performed a solo in front of the choir loft, he just had to take notice. The beauty of her voice induced a mystical sensation within him, and he felt drawn to her as he studied her face. He waited for the service to end in noisy chaos and made his way through the throng. He worked his way towards Nomsa, who was standing beside a slightly older girl. After the formal greetings, he slid into an animated conversation with them for ten minutes, before asking Nomsa, "why don't you join Sunday school perhaps?"

So, when Nomsa started attending Sunday school, he was the first to become her friend. Their friendship deepened into a love and respect greater than that between a brother and sister, despite the fact that Nomsa's parents were not regular churchgoers.

Like everyone else, Ratidzo noticed this friendship and was exasperated by it. She chided Tichaona, reminding him of his youth and pointing out that Nomsa's parents were heathens, and that he shouldn't get too close or he might become like them. Tichaona was not fooled; he could see that his mother didn't like Nomsa. So when he did not heed her warnings, she was possessed by a violent jealousy that swept away all logic. Unable to ignore the situation, she told Edward about the friendship, exaggerating it to the point of making him believe that Tichaona was taking the path of unbelievers.

Edward was greatly disturbed by this, and his reaction was instantaneous. He made arrangements to send Tichaona to St Anne's Mission, where he had grown up. When he told Tichaona what he had in mind for him, the boy knew where the edict was coming from. It made a deep and inerasable mark in his subconscious.

Life at St Anne's Mission was almost the same as at St Theresa's Mission – despite the fact that Tichaona had to stick to the school timetable without wavering. He soon made a close friend by the name of Nyasha. They slept in the same dormitory, were in the same class, and shared thoughts on what they held most dear.

Nyasha was a self-disciplined boy, and it was strange that he was a friend to Tichaona, whose character seemed to be a direct contrast to his. Tichaona was hasty to avenge an insult, and as a result was often in trouble with the school authorities for being involved in fights and violence. His attitude was condemned by those who remembered Edward. How the news of his escapades spread to his father, Tichaona didn't know, but Edward wrote him a letter expressing how extremely disturbed he was. In spite of his pride, Tichaona promised to mend his ways, although he knew he did not really mean it.

One day, one of Edward's parishioners by the name of Tarisai asked Edward if he could help her cousin, Albert, who had been in jail for arson for almost thirteen years, during which period he had lost the woman of his dreams and their child. His compound in the village had been taken by the village head, and his livestock had been shared out among his relatives. He wanted to rebuild his life, but he had nowhere to go. Tarisai wanted to help him, but her husband refused to take him in. She asked friends if they could at least give him a place to stay, to no avail. So at last she decided to ask Edward to take him in, and he agreed despite Ratidzo's tight-lipped disapproval.

Albert came to the Tazvitya home a week later. He was in his early thirties, handsome as an opera star and as thin as a famine victim. When Ratidzo opened the front door, she was flabbergasted to realise that this ex-convict happened to be the love of her teenage years. He had impregnated her, and had promised to marry her and to love her forever, but his arrest had left her with no choice but to get married to someone else – Edward. As they were arguing over Ratidzo's betrayal, Edward walked into the room to welcome Albert.

The few weeks that followed were like a torment to Ratidzo. She felt like a prisoner in her own home. She no longer felt comfortable in Edward's arms when Albert was around, and couldn't do anything properly because Albert's stare demolished her calm. So many times, Albert asked her about their love baby, and Ratidzo couldn't tell him anything. Meanwhile Edward regaled Albert with tales of the son he thought was his own. Day after day and week after week, Ratidzo found it increasingly hard to resist the temptation of loving Albert again.

When Tichaona came home for the holidays, Albert often stared surreptitiously at the smaller replica of his own features when they sat in the same room or exchanged polite conversation. Ratidzo meanwhile made sure that the two were never alone together, even preventing any conversation between them whenever possible.

A few weeks after Tichaona had returned to school, Ratidzo caught a fever and lay in bed for several days. Edward cancelled most of his duties in order to take care of her, and when she was well enough, he returned to work after Albert had promised to look after her. The former lovebirds could resist each other no longer and they started having an affair.

One day, Edward asked Ratidzo if she would lead a group of churchwomen in taking care of Gogo Mwanaka, a frail elderly woman who was past seventy and lived alone. She needed to be clothed and bathed, and to have food cooked for her. To Edward's surprise, his wife refused. "I don't think I'll be able to do that kind of work."

"This is not a question of what you can or can't do. You have to play your role as the preacher's wife."

"Role or no role, I certainly have a right to decide what

99

is right for me. I'm sick and tired of being pushed around like a wheelbarrow. Rati this, Rati that! Please give me a break!"

Edward was astonished by his wife's reaction.. From that day, he became increasingly silent and resentful, neither speaking to Ratidzo nor acknowledging her presence.

Their daughters became aware of the coldness between their parents, and longed for Tichaona's presence as their spokesman. When he came home for the holidays, they told him about the family problem.

Meanwhile, Gogo Mwanaka had died. After her funeral, as the procession of mourners headed back to their homes, Ratidzo confided in Tarisai about her secret lover, in the hope that she would understand, as she was Albert's relative.

After a moment of silence, Tarisai simply said,"In other words, you're actually having an affair behind Edward's back."

"Can't you understand that he was my first...?"

"In whichever way it happened, I merely think that you should deal with Albert's issue in the proper way, because there is no other way."

Unfortunately, the news did not stop there. Tarisai told her aunt, and her aunt gleefully spread the news throughout the church. Within weeks, the Tazvitya family problem was common knowledge. A lot was said, and it was very shameful to see Edward lose his dignity in front of the whole mission. Edward tried to turn a deaf ear to the open gossip, but inside he was breaking into pieces. His self-confidence dissolved and even when he switched on his smile, his eyes betrayed his sadness.

In November 1958, Ratidzo discovered that she was

pregnant. When she told Albert, he was overwhelmed and wanted to tell Edward immediately, but Ratidzo protested. Three weeks later, Ratidzo decided to leave Edward. She wanted to stay for the sake of their children, but because of her pregnancy, she felt she had to choose Albert. When she announced her intention to leave, Edward persuaded her to stay, and asked for forgiveness for his coldness, earnestly promising to do whatever was necessary to be at peace with her. She felt crushed and helpless. She didn't know what to do.

The following day, she told Albert she had decided to stay with Edward and that she intended to end her pregnancy. Albert lost his temper with her, and as the two were having a noisy row, Edward walked in to fetch his Bible, which he had forgotten in the house.

When he demanded an explanation for the row, Albert told him the whole truth. Edward simply froze. The blood drained from his features, leaving them ashen with shock. Although the resemblance between Tichaona and Albert was obvious, Edward denied that he was Albert's son. As Ratidzo tried to explain, he howled out his anger and outrage.

"Shut up! You wicked Jezebel! You harbinger of ill-fortune," he snarled. "Leave my house this minute and don't you ever set foot here again!"

After Ratidzo and Albert had left the house together, Edward cried in the silent spaces of his soul. He had been painfully humiliated and was unable to concentrate on God's work. He tried to pray, but felt recriminations rather than gratitude pressing against his lips. No matter how hard he tried to suppress the pain that Ratidzo had inflicted, it turned out to be too much to bear alone.

Finally, in a suicidal rage, Edward threw himself backwards off a ladder and broke his neck. When his daughters found him, he was already dead.

After the funeral, Father Bob approached Ratidzo (who had to return to mourn her husband) and said in a low and controlled voice, "I know it's too soon for you to decide, but I was thinking that perhaps the girls could continue their education at St Anne's Mission, and the mission will cover their educational expenses." Ratidzo whispered. "It's okay."

"And when you're stronger, you can still continue with your husband's work."

Father Bob waited for Ratidzo to respond, but a full minute passed without a word from her. Then she shook her head sorrowfully. "I want to return to the village."

Almost three weeks later, the girls joined Tichaona at St Anne's Mission. Tichaona was quieter, passive in conversations and laughter with other students, but he still spoke normally, even though he never spoke of his father's death. Only Nyasha knew how deeply it pierced his heart, and how he suffered nightmares, but he never dared to refer to the terrible loss his friend had suffered.

As the school holidays drew near, Albert made it clear that he was not going to look after another man's children. Ratidzo therefore asked her mother if she could take care of the children.

When the Tazvitya children went to their mother's village for the holidays, their grandmother told them that their mother was away visiting relatives, in the hope that her daughter would come up with some way of telling them their true circumstances and Tichaona's true identity.

For the next two weeks, they lived the village life, fetching water from a well, pounding corn in a mortar, working in the fields with their grandparents, gathering firewood and doing other activities. Sometimes they found the life rather monotonous, and Tichaona quickly discovered the only way to cope with the boredom was by taking long walks.

One day, Tichaona took a walk with his cousin, Milton. And as he denigrated Ratidzo for abandoning her children, Milton let the cat out of the bag. Tichaona was deeply shocked. At the same time, all the gossip about his mother, and his father's death, began to make sense to him. Throughout the walk back to the village, he was unusually calm, sometimes twisting his mouth as if he was solving a difficult mathematical problem. He kept telling himself that he was going to show her. She had caused his father's death. After the evening meal, he left his mother's village to accomplish his mission. On his arrival at the new homestead, he stood still at the entrance, taking it all in.

He got to the cattle kraal, went past chickens foraging around the yard, past children playing, and heard laughter. He was still standing, his hatred like an affliction, when his mother came out of a hut holding some plates. She turned her gaze towards the entrance, placed her plates on the ground and approached him in the failing light, her eyes brightening with pleasure. "Ticha –"

"You murderer, you witch – you killed him!"
She was puzzled. "What are you talking about?" She stepped forward and tried to touch him, but he pushed her and she stumbled backwards.

"You killed my father! I hate you for it!"
"How could you say that to me?"

"You killed him! You killed him! You bitch!" Tichaona cried out in anger.

"We can talk about this, my child."

He didn't want to be her child any longer. Like a man possessed by demons, he threw stones at her. Ratidzo screamed as she collapsed to the ground, blood from her head trickling down her face. "You've chosen the path of a prodigal son, nothing you ever do will prosper," she cried, wincing in pain. "I swear it on your life and the nine months I carried you!"

As Tichaona continued to stone his mother, Albert rushed forward to stop him. He tried to reason with him, but because of his volatile temper he would not listen. Tichaona ran back to the village, and no one could reason with him, even though Ratidzo had sustained serious head injuries. She died a few weeks later, and he was not even bothered. He didn't realise how great the taboo he had broken was.

Tichaona was taken to St Anne's orphanage, where he stayed until he was ready to return home. However, he refused to do so. Albert tried to persuade him, to no avail. After the school holidays, Ropafadzo returned to school a week late without Rutendo, and when Tichaona asked about her whereabouts, he was told that she had run away, and no one knew where she had gone.

At seventeen, Tichaona managed to acquire a scholarship to study abroad. He often wrote to Ropafadzo and Nomsa. A few years later, Nomsa stopped replying to his letters and Ropafadzo told him that she had married another man.

Tichaona's life became a dark void, without meaning or purpose. No other girl replaced Nomsa. After Ropafadzo finished secondary school, she trained as a nurse. A few years later, she got married to Temba, a primary school teacher, and together they had two children.

Fifteen years later, Tichaona returned to his country, where he got a good job. But any little money that came to hand simply went down the drain;, every relationship he had with a woman ended badly; in fact, everything he got involved in looked wonderful at the beginning, but.ended in disaster

Tichaona got married to Tsitsi and had three children with her. At first their life together was exciting and seemed to be headed for success. However, when he was nearly forty, he fell in love with Muchaneta, a single mother of two. When Tsitsi became aware of this, they had a number of fights, and Tichaona ran off to Muchaneta in defiance. He abandoned his family, and Tsitsi had to struggle to keep their children in school.

A few years later, Tichaona lost his job after being accused of theft. He struggled to get another job, but with no luck. He sold all that he had to support his concubine, and when he was left with nothing Muchaneta chased him away. He thought of his mother's bitter words, with great misery, and returned to his wife, Tsitsi, to beg her for forgiveness. In the face of their children's disapproval, she granted it.

In the summer of 2003, Tsitsi had a heart attack and died on her way to hospital. A month after the funeral, Tsitsi's relatives took everything – the house and the furniture – leaving Tichaona with nowhere to stay. His children turned their backs on him. He stayed on the streets for almost two years until a stranger took him to the social welfare office. And that was how he came to be brought to New Hope old people's home.

Tichaona paused as he shed some tears accompanied by sobs. "I'm sorry for who I am. The prodigal son in the Bible was given a second chance, but I never got that chance."

Writer's Block

By Helen Moffett

On the hotel terrace overlooking milky Lake Victoria,
Winnie, slim at sixty, elegant, prayerful,
turns the talk to writer's block.
She cannot make progress with her novel.
Then, with no sense of non sequiter,
she speaks of life under Idi Amin,
and the soldiers' long reign of terror.
"Perhaps I should write it," she says.
"But who will care? Everyone has forgotten.
Besides, I do not want to remember."
There is a pause. The kites hover.
And as sudden as the downpour in the hot afternoons,
her words come: the story of the roadblock,
how the soldiers told her and her friend,
"You ladies, come with us. Driver, carry on."
It was dusk. The driver risked his life,
refusing point-blank to leave without them.
For two hours, they pleaded in Swahili.
For two hours, guns waved, threats were made.
Then suddenly, it was over. Go, go,
said the soldiers, losing interest.
Winnie made some excuse for her lateness that night.
She never told her husband how close she came
to never coming home at all.
     Another day, her four-year-old son

ran screaming to the bathroom
where she stood washing herself:
"Soldiers! Soldiers are here!"
Her only thought: "Lord, let me not die naked."
The house was searched for guns –
saucepans, books, panties, all
excavated and tossed about –
mattresses slit, suitcases hacked at.
Baulked, empty-handed, the soldiers
chased them out of their despoiled home:
"Go to church, now, hurry!
Do not run to warn your neighbours."

      There is another pause. Kingwa,
at twenty-five, is indignant – the rest of us, older,
know how madness can surge into the sweetest day.

In Another Country

By Helen Moffett

In other countries, I become a different person.
In Uganda, I drink beer after Tusker beer,
and in Barbados, home-made herb rum.
In Alaska, I drive a four-by-four.
In Ireland, I stick out my thumb.
In Greece, I share a room with strangers.
And everywhere, I get up before dawn,
climbing out of windows if I have to,
scrambling to catch first light.

On the sacred isle of Iona, adrift in the Hebrides,
I walk along a beach, confessing
clutching the hand of an impossible man
I have known for all of three days.
And I skydive into love, freefalling,
wind whistling past my ears.
A day later, I kiss him
in the middle of the night,
in the middle of a storm,
spray wet on our faces,
caught in the boom of a kettledrum.

At home, I never do any of these things.
I'm a white wine girl who doesn't see sunrise.
My car is small and second-hand.

I seldom take risks.
And while I might fall in love,
I no longer jump out of planes,
hurtle into the heart of the wind.

But maybe I should. Live in another country.

Gift Of A Letter

By Lilian Tindyebwa

5 November 2008

Dear Zawadi

How are you today? I hear Kenya is such a lovely country. You have become such a friend that I cannot wait to write to you each day. My struggles to get familiar with Internet use have paid off in this way.

My friend Zawadi, I remember last time I told you about the madam I work for; she has this habit of leaving the house late to go to work. That's why I did not send you a letter yesterday. She delayed so much that it was too late for me to run out and send it.

And today was almost the same. I got impatient! I kept praying that she would leave. At one point I thought that maybe the clock in the living-room was slow, so I switched on the radio just to be sure, and guess what, it was still seven thirty, half an hour left for her to leave the house! I made myself busy with the housework so that she would not notice my disquiet.

She finally walked out at 8.15 am, with her twin daughters Nana and Barbie trailing behind her. Did I tell you about Nana and Barbie? They are sweet little angels aged four years and they go to nursery school. She drops them off on her way to work and she picks them up at lunch-time.

When she left the house I heaved a sigh of relief, because

I had started to suffer lapses of concentration. That was how I burnt Nana's pretty little uniform. It would have been fine, but the little girl loves it so much – I think it's what makes her aware that she is now in school. I looked at the tiny dress and there was a big V- shaped hole that seemed to cover half the upper part of the dress. Zawadi, I felt so terrible seeing her cry, and you should have seen the way Madam looked at me! She was obviously making a superhuman effort not to release a barrage of insults at me, but her eyes said it all. I told her I was very sorry, but she just walked away without a single word, leaving me to stew in my guilt.

Then I got so worried, Zawadi, because I thought that she might send me away. The idea of losing this job made me tremble. My mind came to a standstill. Has your mind ever come to a standstill, Zawadi? Then I saw that the table with the breakfast things was still not cleared, so I decided to clear them. My hands were shaking and I almost dropped the tray.

You see, my friend, I really need this money very much badly! I cannot afford to lose this job. Despite the fact that being a nanny is one of the most despised jobs, with name tags like "housegirl" and "domestic help", for me it's a godsend, whatever it may be called. Do not ask yourself why. The reason is simple, I have somewhere to stay! Oh I know madam needs me too!

You should see her, Zawadi, the madam, I mean! She is very tall and dark-skinned, and one of the prettiest people I have ever seen in my life. Not only that, she is also clever. At thirty-two, she already has a PhD in economics. You should hear her talking, you would wish she was your sister or your mother – either would be all right with me. I still can't believe that some lousy man let her down. What did he want her to be like?

But anyway, that makes two of us. It also makes her a single mother of twins who needs the help of a nanny or "housegirl", whatever she chooses to call me, as long as she pays me and gives me shelter.

Zawadi, I am so happy to have you as a friend, and in the coming days I will be telling you in pieces what my life has been like. I say "pieces" because I am shattered and it is all in pieces.

One thing I know for sure, I am glad to have someone to talk to without fear. I have so much to say from years of packed silence; that explains why I fret when I fail to get time to write to you. But I like my work. I love madam's twin daughters, Nana and Barbie. They remind me of my own baby. She is pretty like them. I called her Petua Kirabo. Petua was my grandmother who brought me up and Kirabo is my name, so we share it, and just like yours, it means "gift". I miss my baby so much, I cry myself to sleep every night.

I write to you from a small Internet café near where we live. It's appropriately named Salaama. Yes, I do find peace when I write to you.

Zawadi, I have never been able to tell anyone about the absurd drama that took place when the authorities of the school I was attending found out that I was pregnant. I was about to sit my Primary Leaving Examinations. That was two years ago. But I cannot forget how everyone treated me. You would think that I had rabies or something worse! My poor grandmother, after pleading that I should at least be allowed to complete these exams, was instructed to come with me to school every day and wait for me to finish the papers so that she could take me away with her! Zawadi, was I going to contaminate anybody just because I was pregnant?

In all this, they did not try to ask about which man was responsible. It made me realise that this was a grand plan to protect him.

My grandmother told me not to worry, that my examinations were more important at that point than revealing the truth about this man, who was among those who were leading in demonising me.

My grandmother is now looking after my baby. I am working so that I can go to high school and support them both. Zawadi, piles of dirty baby clothes await me. I have to finish washing them, then prepare lunch. So I will sign off.

Peace and love from Kirabo

8 November 2008

Dear Kirabo

I have just seen your letter and I am crying as I read it over and over again. Kirabo, I thank the stars that brought us together. We have not met physically, but through these pages I see you, I touch you, I greet you, I walk with you and live with you.

Kirabo, we are so much alike. And just like you, I am glad to find someone to tell the truth, the deepest truths about my life.

You see my friend, everything that has ever happened to me, ever since I can remember, has always been someone else's idea.

One day I came home from school and I found people at my home. I was just told I had to go with them, and that one of them was to be my husband. I pleaded with my father, my own loving father, whom I loved and whose favourite child I had always been. I was sure he would listen and change his mind. I blamed the uncles who were also sitting there in their funny old coats. I approached him and fell before him and cried. When I was young he would never allow anybody to beat me, and I believed that my tears would move him to change his mind.

Kirabo, whoever said that people can change in a day must have been right. My father was no longer the father I used to know. He had changed. When did he learn to be indifferent to the tears of his little "gift"? Had he become stone-deaf?

"Papa," I pleaded, "please let me finish school, I have only two years left to do my O-levels," I reminded him as if he could have forgotten. He stared at me for a minute, as if he was considering the options. I cried even more. Then he spoke, his voice like that of a wild beast: "Get away before I beat you in front of everyone!"

I got up quickly because I knew that he meant what he said. In brief, he refused to listen to me. He got angry and threatened me and told me he had already accepted their bride price, and that I was trying to be a useless girl if I did not fetch money for him through the bride price.

I went to my mother and told her: "Mama, help me. Hide me or kill me, but do not give me to these strange men." At first I wondered whether she had heard me because she just sat there, as if lifeless, tears just rolling down her cheeks. Then I realised that she was incapable, absolutely powerless to change the decisions taken by my father and my uncles.

Then I went mad. I screamed and threw stones; then I ran towards the river, ready to drown myself. The band of uncles dressed to give away the bride and those dressed to receive the bride threw down their walking sticks and ran after me. I ran the race of my life, knowing that I would not drown myself, but would hide and leave the village instead. They would not have caught me if I had not met some people coming towards our home. They grabbed me, thinking that they were doing me a favour, because they thought I had probably run mad and in grabbing me, they were saving my life. One huge man held my legs, another held my arms and another one held my body. I gave up because I was pinned down. It did not matter how much I wriggled and shouted and hurled abuse at them, they would not release me. I gave up. That was how I left my home.

116

Now I live here in Isiolo, with this strange family. At seventeen, I have two children, a boy called Moses, and the girl, Njiri. Their lives will be different from mine, I will see to that.

Kirabo, you know, I secretly started studying computer. That is how I am able to write to you. I walk three kilometres to the nearest trading centre, where I have been able to get someone to teach me privately. I do this twice a week or else I would be writing to you every day. I deceive my mother-in-law that I am in the garden, or at times I say that one of the children is sick and I come with him or her.

Today I came with Njiri. She is sitting next to me, cuddling a toy as I write to you. My lesson for today has ended.

Do you know what life with my husband is like, Kirabo? I do not know whether to call it a circus or a horror film. It is probably a mixture of both.

This was not my dream, Kirabo. I dreamt of places, of a career, of a life full of excitement, but not this! Do you know that I have co-wives? And that my husband is old enough to be my father, and some of my co-wives are old enough to be my mothers?

We all live together in one compound like a herd of goats. What irritates me most is when these women try to boss me around. I will have none of that stuff, and I have made it very clear to them. So they hate me because they think that I have no respect for them. I have tried to understand them, but it has been a bit hard for me. They are trapped, Kirabo. I wish I could help them, but it is not possible. Culture has been misread and misused to benefit a few and hurt others. It is sad. So even if I gave them respect, it would never solve any of their problems.

As for my husband, allow me to tell you about him next time, because his is a long, long story. Now I have to go before my mother-in-law gets suspicious.

Write soon.

Till next time,
Peace and love from your friend
Zawadi

I Still Remember

By Betty Mukashema

I'll live to remember you all.
Hilda, that beam is not be forgotten.
I'll live to remember Lillian's motherly love.
I can't forget lovely Olivia with the big manuscript, age not withstanding!
You really were an inspiration to us all.
Colleen I swear to you,
I'll remember to keep the pen moving, a word from your mouth.
Please Philo,
Keep the cock crowing and remind Margaret to keep her love for the one she loves.
Connie, so close to Sophie, the law is against you guys.
Watch out!
I hope Winnie drives home as early as possible to escape the awful moment of jam on Kampala Streets.
Regards to Kingwa and Yemodish from the chilly breeze of the Nile waters.
It was pretty exciting!
We trekked an incomplete journey without you two!
Mbeo, I liked that figure of a spot-on African mother.
I am in the family way too at least psychologically.
Yaba, I liked that proper African style.
We ought to have gone the Ghanaian way.
Helen, you actually made it! You passionately healed all our

souls.

We swear to make you happy with our pens.

By the way, still asking, "Where do broken hearts go?"

Hoping to hear from you all, soonest.

Long live Mother Hen!

Long live FEMRITE AFRICA!

The Curse Of The Red Pen

Public Lecture presented at Makerere University, during the FEMRITE Regional African Women Writers Residency 20th November 2008

Presented by Dr Helen Moffet
Facilitator of the Residence

Dear friends, colleagues and fellow writers, thank you for your presence here. I especially thank "Mother Hen", Mary Karooro Okurut, who has come directly from a long day in Parliament. Thanks to all at Makerere University who have been our friends, and who have given us the benefit of their wisdom and insights – and thanks to the university for hosting this performance and address. Thanks to FEMRITE, not just for a wonderful residency, but for giving us the opportunity to share our work with you; and myself the privilege of addressing you all.

My presentation is titled: *The Curse of the Red Pen: Editing Women Writers in Anglophone Post-Colonial Africa.* I was at Johannesburg airport on my way to Uganda trying to think of a snappy title for this lecture, when I uncapped my red pen, and it exploded in my hands – all over my clothing, my luggage and my papers. I had to get on the plane with red-spotted hands. Hence "The Curse of the Red Pen" as a title for my thoughts on my experiences as an editor of women writers in Africa, and what I have learnt from these. Most of those I work with are academics, although increasingly, I deal with creative writers as well.

The first thing that I have learned, if I may generalise, is that Africa is a fount of rich creativity, of gripping stories and innovative art forms, at a time when Western and Northern academic and publishing institutions seem to have grown formulaic, inflexible, irrelevant or simply dull.

As a South African, I am very much aware that with both the arrogance and enthusiasm of youth, our very young democracy has bounced ahead with announcing the African Renaissance so beloved of our former president Thabo Mbeki. Well, his ideals have been crushed, to the blushes of a nation. And when, at a public reading in Atlanta USA in 2007, Nobel laureate Wole Soyinka was asked what he thought of this African Renaissance, his pithy response was not one that can be repeated in polite company.

Yet I can see a future in which Africa becomes a cultural powerhouse, feeding the world with stories, dreams, visions, fables, films, plays, poetry and more. Yes, we know that many publishing houses in Africa have fallen prey to general infrastructural collapse, as has happened to Zimbabwe`s once thriving independent publishing institution. And yet Zimbabwe has gone on hosting an annual book fair – a book fair in the midst of all that hunger and chaos? What madness, what courage, what need to honour stories must propel them! Yes, we know that those publishing houses that do survive in Africa are educational publishers that produce textbooks and prescribed books for our schools, and their requirements are narrow, and not necessary suited to creative innovation. And yet a number of our authors, myself included, feed our writing habit by writing a textbook or two to buy us a brief spell of financial security and space.

But possibly our greatest ally in terms of what I believe is an African cultural explosion to happen is the Internet. Many grumble about this, arguing that communities in Africa have far more pressing needs – clean water, clean energy, food security – and of course I agree. But high-speed Internet access is either coming to Africa's urban centres, or it has already arrived. In South Africa, we are currently laying an undersea cable that will enhance the connectivity of the entire southern African region and beyond. This makes options for distributing, sharing, and even publishing our stories, our songs, our film clips, far more immediate, far more accessible, and very much cheaper. Instead of sending our manuscripts to a publisher and then waiting months and months for a reply (which is all too often a rejection), we can publish our work and cultural productions in cyberspace, in open access forms, for very little money.

However, post-colonial Africa remains haunted by fear of the red pen – a pen all too often wielded by a settler, a missionary, a magistrate, a colonial official. We still hand our ideas over to outsiders far too readily, and submit too hastily to their judgement. The African historian Paul Zeleza has said that while the West might have innovative theories, paradigms and theoretical models for processing data, it is poor in raw data – every topic has been exhaustively researched. Africa, however, is an extraordinarily rich field for researchers; it is here that answers to the most pressing concerns of the twenty-first century will be found. The HIV/Aids pandemic, the environmental devastation of the planet we all call home, religious fundamentalism, the inexplicable torrent of violence against women and children, and above all, the impulses that move communities to clash in civil war – the keys to unlock all these puzzles are to be found here, must be found here, if we are to survive.

But what happens? We allow a tide of young foreign students and researchers to settle on us like locusts, carrying our stories, our ideas, our research back to places like Yale and Harvard, where they are published in international journals to the advantage of the careers of others. (This is of course not to suggest that such partnerships may not be valuable – but then they must be partnerships in which we lead the way, set the terms, or are at least are equal.)

When students from Stockholm and Stanford come to interview me about my work on sexual violence in post-apartheid South Africa, and I ask why they are so interested, they say they want to "make a contribution". I respond: "That's excellent news. Now please join the Peace Corps." Or I suggest that they first spend a year learning a local language and learning to drive in local conditions; and once they have acquired practical, useful skills, that they spend a year working for one of our NGOs. Then it might be appropriate to go home and write up their findings, burnishing their resumes. But we have to halt the process whereby we are simply a source of data and local expertise to be mined and analysed by scores of visitors to Africa – some of whom are here for only a matter of weeks.

But this means that we must take responsibility for our own dates, our resources, and our stories. We must be the ones showcasing our literature, presenting and analysing our own data. And many of us are indeed doing this – think for instance, of the cutting-edge research and writing being done by women such as Dr Sylvia Tamale from Uganda and Yaba Badoe from Ghana, both present here. But we need to be savvy and strategic if we are to avoid the syndrome I call "inviting Africa to the party and turning her away at the door". We are baffled when we submit our work to Western and Northern publishers, for international and even pan-African prizes, only to be rebuffed. Or in the case of prizes for African writers, to find that the South Africans or the Nigerians have won yet again.

We must learn to be professional in the way we present ourselves in a global world; we must decipher the unwritten codes that act as forms of gate-keeping. It is not enough to write, to tell our stories, to share our knowledge; we must also learn to edit our work, to proofread it, to market it, shape it to meet the needs of an international audience, if that's what it takes. Merit is unfortunately no longer enough in a world of branded goods – but we must remember that the one thing we are not short of is merit.

And this is where fear of the red pen takes its toll. When we hear "no" from a publisher, a funder, an employer, we assume that this is because of lack of merit, and we meekly accept the big red cross of disapproval. Or we look to an outside editor, or expert, someone to whom we can hand our work. But we cannot afford to abdicate either our ownership of our work, or our responsibility for it.

We have to train ourselves, commit to skills transfer, and work as hard at our professional presentation as we do our research and writing. We have to acknowledge that if we write in English, we are using a settler lingua franca that for many of us, is not a mother tongue. Many of us translate every thought, every image, before we put pen to paper or finger to keyboard. Rather than being discouraged, we must acknowledge and allow time for this process. But we must also celebrate our power to adapt our dreams into stories that can be enjoyed by many. We must strive to reflect idiomatically our multilingual heritage, even as we write in one English – and it can be done. So I urge you, pick up the red pen. Own it; use it as a tool; wield it as a weapon; and embrace it as a friend.

Notes On Residence Participants

Alal Sophie Brenda from Uganda holds a Bachelor of Laws Degree from Makerere University. Alal is a very talented young woman whose writing career is on the rise. She won the Second Prize in the first Beverly Nambozo Poetry Award 2009. Alal's works written during the residence and read at the Public Reading were very original and definitive of her voice, a voice that takes commonplace themes and turns them into masterpieces.

Badoe   Yaba is a Ghanaian-British documentary film maker and journalist. a graduate of King's College, Cambridge, she worked as a civil servant in Ghana before becoming a general trainee with the BBC. She has taught in Spain and Jamaica and is presently a Visiting Scholar at the Institute of African Studies at the University of Ghana. Badoe is a published author with short stories in Critical Quarterly and African Love Stories. Her first novel, *True Murder*, made a remarkable debut on the literary scene.

Bekele Yemodish is a journalist from Ethiopia. Her story written during the residence and read during the public reading examines the position of a sexually abused girl-child in the face of an equally abusive law system. Yeomodish's story, unfortunately not part of this anthology, inspired the poem titled You are One by Hilda Twongyeirwe. Yemodish is the Chairperson of the Women Writers Association of Ethiopia.

HiggsColleen was born in Kimberley, South Africa. She now leaves in Cape Town. Colleen is a published writer with poems and stories in different literary magazines and anthologies. She is the author of **Halfborn Woman**. She champions the cause for writers especially emerging writers and those writing in African Languages. 1n 2007, Colleen's dedication to creative writing led her to establish Modjaji Books Press, which she describes as a small publishing house. One of Modjaji maiden publications was short listed for the Sunday Times Fiction Prize, which is South Africa's most prestigious Literary Award.

Jembere Olivia is one of Zimbabwe's young writers struggling to find their literary voices in the middle of Zimbabwe's political unrest. She is one of the youngest members of Zimbabwe Women Writers Association (ZWWA). Despite the different challenges, Olivia has managed to complete her first novel for which she is currently looking for a publisher.

Kingwa Kamencu comes from Kenya. During her first year at University Kingwa won the second prize of the National Book Development Council of Kenya for her novella To Grasp at a Star. Later the same novella won the youth category of the Jomo Kenyatta Prize for Literature, which is Kenya's most prestigious literary prize. The only girl in a family of boys is one of Kenya's youngest Award Winning authors. She is currently pursuing a Masters Degree in Literature, at the University of Nairobi. Kingwa writes widely in different genres. Her biggest influences in poetry are local poets; Muthoni Garland, Bantu Mwaura, Shailja Patel, Philo Ikonya among others

Mbeo Mastidia hails from Tanzania. She is a member of the Tanzania Writers Association and she serves on the executive committee of the Women Writers Branch. She is a published writer and editor but she has been writing only in Swahili. Her maiden writings in English were conceived at the Regional Writers Residence, one of which, made it into Pumpkin Seeds and other Gifts.

Dr. Helen Moffet is a freelance writer, academic, editor and trainer. She has lectured all over the world on the social, political and cultural dimensions of cricket, and has co-produced two documentary films on cricket and nation-building in South Africa. She is a published poet of remarkable courage in the way she deals with her themes. She worked as a Research Fellow at the African Gender Institute. She holds a PhD from the English Department at University of Cape Town, where she taught for eight years. She has held prestigious fellowships at Princeton University, Mount Holyoke College and has been a Rockefeller Associate at University of Cape Town's African Gender Institute. She has also worked in publishing, and was Oxford University Press's academic editor for four years. Helen has authored a number of books both fiction and creative non fiction.

Mukashema Betty hails from Rwanda. She is an aspiring young writer who has mainly been writing for the media . Her maiden fiction publications were written during the Regional Residence which Betty described as a dream come true. Betty is a Teacher by Profession and she teaches at Kagarama Secondary School in Kigali. Betty's current dream is to help Rwanda establish a women writers association that will connect Rwandan Women writers to other women writers in Africa. Betty is passionate about cultural identity in relation to change.

Munyarugerero Winnie is a published author whose writings mainly explore the position of the woman and the girl-child in Uganda. Her short stories and articles are published in different anthologies, magazines and Newspapers. She is especially interested in the education of the girl-child and issues concerning women and children. Winnie is a teacher by profession and she holds a Bachelor of Arts Degree in English and French.

Nabweru Philomena Rwabukuku is a Ugandan teacher of English Language and Literature in English. She holds a Bachelor of Arts Degree in Literature and Psychology. She is currently studying for a Master's Degree in Counselling. Philomena is a published writer with short stories and poems published in different anthologies. She recites and performs oral literature and is very interested in issues of women and children. She has written several articles on growing up and parenting in different magazines.

Ntakalimaze Margaret hails from Uganda. She has published a number of poems and short stories in different anthologies. She is very passionate about women and children's issues. Currently, she is the Founding Coordinator of Uganda Women and Children Organisation. Margaret participated in the Okot p'Bitek Memorial festival in 1991 and her poem in Praise of Okot p'Bitek was recognized among the best presentations.

Obonyo Connie hails from Uganda. She holds a Bachelor of Laws Degree. She writes mainly for The Observer Newspaper but she has also published poems in *Today You will Understand* and in *Painted Voices Vol. 1.*

Tindyebawa Lillian was born in South-Western Uganda. She is a published writer whose poems and short stories are published in different anthologies. Lillian's instant success as a writer came with her first novel for young adults **Recipe for Disaster** when it was recommended as a supplementary reader for all secondary schools in Uganda. She holds a Bachelor of Arts Degree and a Masters Degree in Literature. Lillian has also published three books for children.

Twongyeirwe Hilda Rutagonya hails from Uganda. She has published short stories and poems in anthologies and literary journals. Her children's book **Fina the Dancer** was highly commended by National Book Trust of Uganda Literary Awards, as an outstanding piece of literature for children. She has written several children's books in her local language. Her unpublished play titled **Demobilised** was performed at the Uganda National Cultural Centre in 1997. Hilda was honoured to be one of the First Judges of the Beverley Nambozo Poetry Award 2009. Hilda holds a Diploma in Education, a Degree in Social Sciences and a Masters Degree in Public Administration and Management from Makerere University. Currently she is the Coordinator of Uganda Women Writers Association and she is working to establish a network of women writers associations in Africa.

Other FEMRITE Publications.

Anthologies:

A Woman's Voice	- *Ugandan Women Writers.*
Words From A Granary	- *Ugandan Women Writers.*
Tears of Hope	- *FEMRITE scriptwriters.*
Directory of Ugandan Writers	- *FEMRITE*
Gifts of Harvest	- *Ugandan Women Writers.*
I Dare to Say	- *FEMRITE.*
In their Own Words	- *FEMRITE.*
Today you will understand	- *FEMRITE Writers.*
Farming Ashes	- *FEMRITE Writers.*
Beyond the Dance	- *FEMRITE Writers.*

Novels:

Memoirs of a Mother	- *Ayeta Anne Wangusa.*
The Invisible Weevil	- *Mary Karooro Okurut.*
Silent Patience	- *Jane Kaberuka.*
A Season no Mirth	- *Regina Amollo.*
Secrets no More	- *Goretti Kyomuhendo.*
Cassandra	- *Violet Barungi.*
Shockwaves Across the Ocean	- *Jocelyn Ekochu Bananuka.*

Poetry:

The African Saga	- *Susan Kiguli.*
No Hearts at Home	- *Christine Oryema Lalobo.*
Painted Voices Vol. I & II	- *FEMRITE Writers.*